A PENGUIN MYSTERY

# THE THIEF OF VENICE

Jane Langton's Homer Kelly mysteries include *Dead as a Dodo* and *The Shortest Day*, among many others. She lives in Lincoln, Massachusetts.

# THE

# Thief of Venice

## A HOMER KELLY MYSTERY

*Illustrations by the author*

# Jane Langton

PENGUIN BOOKS

PENGUIN BOOKS

Published by the Penguin Group
Penguin Putnam Inc., 375 Hudson Street,
New York, New York 10014, U.S.A.
Penguin Books Ltd, 27 Wrights Lane, London W8 5TZ, England
Penguin Books Australia Ltd, Ringwood, Victoria, Australia
Penguin Books Canada Ltd, 10 Alcorn Avenue,
Toronto, Ontario, Canada M4V 3B2
Penguin Books (N.Z.) Ltd, 182–190 Wairau Road,
Auckland 10, New Zealand

Penguin Books Ltd, Registered Offices:
Harmondsworth, Middlesex, England

First published in the United States of America by Viking Penguin,
a member of Penguin Putnam Inc. 1999
Published in Penguin Books 2000

1  3  5  7  9  10  8  6  4  2

Copyright © Jane Langton, 1999
All rights reserved

Illustrations by the author

Grateful acknowledgment is made for permission to reprint an excerpt from
Dante's *The Divine Comedy, Volume 2: Purgatory*, translated by Dorothy L. Sayers
(Penguin Books). By permission of David Higham Associates.

PUBLISHER'S NOTE

This is a work of fiction. Names, characters, places, and incidents are either
the product of the author's imagination or are used fictitiously, and any
resemblance to actual persons, living or dead, business establishments,
events, or locales is entirely coincidental.

THE LIBRARY OF CONGRESS HAS CATALOGUED
THE HARDCOVER EDITION AS FOLLOWS:
Langton, Jane.
The thief of Venice/Jane Langton: illustrations by the author.
p.  cm.
"A Homer Kelly mystery."
ISBN 0-670-88210-0 (hc.)
ISBN 0 14 02.9189 X (pbk.)
I. Title.
PS3562.A515T47    1999
813'.54—dc21        99–54894

Printed in the United States of America
Set in Simoncini Garamond • Designed by Ann Gold

Except in the United States of America, this book is sold subject to the
condition that it shall not, by way of trade or otherwise, be lent, re-sold, hired
out, or otherwise circulated without the publisher's prior consent in any form of
binding or cover other than that in which it is published and without a similar
condition including this condition being imposed on the subsequent purchaser.

*For Laura Lilli*

*The city of Venice is rich in holy relics and the bodies of saints.*
*Faith in their miraculous power is no longer*
*as fervent as in the past,*
*but candles are still lighted before some of them,*
*showing an enduring devotion.*

# CHAPTER 1

✖

*Many novels start with a funeral and end with a wedding. This
one begins with everything at the same time—a robbery,
a proposal of marriage, and a murder.*

✖

Schoolgirls streamed out of the Scuola di Nostra Signora
della Consolazione. They gathered in clots and clusters
and hurried away, chattering and laughing. The last to
come out was a little fat girl. She lingered until the others were
gone, then started home by herself.

"Ursula!" Sister Maddalena stood in the doorway, calling after
her.

The child turned around with a blank face.

Sister Maddalena frowned. "Ursula, did you take money out
of my cash box? Let me see your backpack."

Without a word the little girl untangled herself from the
straps and handed the backpack to Sister Maddalena.

"Humph," said Sister Maddalena, groping inside it. "I'm
sorry to accuse you, Ursula, but you remember that I caught you
stealing before."

Ursula hunched herself into her pack again and walked out of
the schoolyard without a word.

The shop was on the way home. Ursula took the money out
of the pocket of her school uniform and set it on the counter,
*plink, plink,* and pointed to the one she wanted.

The man behind the counter looked at the coins. The child must have known it wasn't enough, she had bought so many before. "Ah, well, it will do. This one is a little chipped."

⌗

# CHAPTER 2

*D*ottoressa Lucia Costanza walked along the Molo from the San Marco vaporetto stop, edging past throngs of tourists and flocks of pigeons. Turning left onto the Piazzetta she strode past the Ducal Palace and the west front of San Marco, not bothering to glance at its fanciful domes and gilded pinnacles. Instead she looked up at the clock tower, where the winged lion of Saint Mark displayed his famous book with its angelic blessing, PAX TIBI MARCE EVANGELISTA MEUS. On the top of the tower she could clearly see the bronze bell-ringers in the metal bearskins that did not quite conceal their private parts.

The big clock told her she was late on her first morning as a newly hired member of the Procuratori di San Marco. Quicening her steps, she turned into the Piazzetta dei Leoncini, whirled past the north side of the basilica, hurried into the Palazzo Patriarcale, sped through the first courtyard, nodded at a stranger loitering at the foot of the stairs, and ran up to her new office.

It was a beautiful office, and Lucia was anxious to deserve it. Closing the door, she went quickly to the window to relish again the view of the second courtyard, with its crazed miscellany of architectural fragments plastered around the imbedded buttress of the basilica.

*"Buongiorno, Dottoressa."*

Lucia twirled around in surprise to see her assistant, Tommaso Bernardi, bowing with formal courtesy.

*"*Oh, *buongiorno,* Signor Bernardi. I didn't see you." She smiled at him, wondering if his bow was ironic. She knew that

he had been a candidate himself for the opening on this prestigious board. He must be disappointed at not becoming the latest in the long line of citizen procurators, stretching back for a thousand years. In the days of the Republic they had worn robes of red silk with velvet stoles. The robes were gone now, and so was the necessity upon investiture to distribute bread to the poor and wine to the gondoliers. But the distinction remained. Lucia hoped Bernardi would not feel a grudge against her, because she needed his advice. He was an old hand. He could teach her the ways of the place.

"Signor Bernardi, I hope you will call me Lucia."

He looked shocked. He did not suggest that she call him Tommaso. He came forward, holding a card between finger and thumb as if it were an oily rag, and dropped it on her desk. "A person wishes to see you."

Lucia glanced at the card. At once she recognized the name. Dottor Samuele Bell was a famous personage in the city, celebrated for his scholarship and for his important position in the Library of Saint Mark.

"Of course, of course. Tell him to come right up." Lucia jumped out of her chair. "I'll tell him myself."

Dismayed, Signor Bernardi stood out of the way as she ran past him. She was halfway down the stairs when her visitor appeared below her, ascending slowly. Lucia hurried down with her hand out. For the rest of his life Sam Bell would remember the broad smile and the welcoming hand.

"I hope," said Lucia, "that the curator of rare books in the Biblioteca Marciana will become a friend and colleague. I'm going to need your help. I need everyone's help. I don't know anything yet."

Sam's tongue failed him. It was hard to believe that this majestic woman could be ignorant of anything. As she turned and walked up with him the rest of the way she said impulsively, "Your exhibition, I'm so eager to see it. Am I too late to apply for the conference?"

"Oh, Dottoressa Costanza, you don't need to apply. You will be our honored guest. And I hope you'll let me give you a tour of the exhibition." He beamed at her, then smiled with less conviction at Signor Bernardi as Lucia introduced him.

*"Molto piacere,"* said Sam politely.

*"Piacere mio,"* said Bernardi, standing his ground.

"Thank you, Signor Bernardi," said Lucia, hoping he would have the intelligence to remove himself.

He did, but only slowly, looking back with suspicion and failing to close the door.

Lucia closed it gently herself, and smiled. "Do sit down and tell me what I can do for you."

Since yesterday Doctor Samuele Bell had been transformed from a reasonable person into a creature of impulse. Nothing mattered anymore. He could do what he liked. He put his hands on Lucia's desk and leaned forward as she sat down. Words came out of his mouth. He said, "Marry me. Please marry me."

There was only the slightest pause, and then Lucia said amiably, "Why, certainly. Oh, well, of course as it happens, I'm married already, but who cares about a little thing like that?" She glanced playfully around the room. "All we need now is a justice of the peace." She grinned at him. "Well, now that we've settled that, sit down and tell me what you're really here for. And please call me Lucia."

He sat down, feeling like a fool. It was all very well to tell himself that nothing mattered, but of course everything did matter. He had blundered into her office and smashed all the delicate china and behaved like an idiot. But Dottoressa Costanza—Lucia!—had forgiven him, she had made a joke of it.

He wanted to fall on his knees. "And you must call me Sam. It's an American nickname, because, you see, my father was an American." He could hear himself dithering. He stopped and began again. "My request is this." He cleared his throat and tried to speak formally, as one important official to another. "I hope you will give me permission to make a scientific examination of the sacred relics in the Treasury of San Marco in order to determine their authenticity. Your predecessor refused to consider the matter. I hope you'll be more open-minded."

"What? You want to examine the relics?" Lucia stared at him openmouthed, then threw back her head and laughed. It was a loud unmusical bray of a laugh. "You want to borrow all the holy relics in the basilica as if it were a public library? Dottor Bell—Sam—you must be mad."

He laughed too. "Well, perhaps insanity runs in my family. But, Dottoressa Lucia, isn't it time someone took a careful look at all those miscellaneous bones and scraps of wood? Where do they come from? The saints' bones, *per esempio,* are some of them from dogs, cats, sheep? Are the pieces of the True Cross just miscellaneous scraps of wood from some carpenter's workshop? Look here, I'm not only a librarian, I've got a degree in natural science. I can tell a human bone from—"

Lucia lifted her hand, smiling. "Well, it's absolutely outrageous, but I'll see what I can do." She turned her head as a saxophone in one of the distant swing bands on the piazza uttered a loud bleat, sending a squadron of pigeons flying up past the window. "Perhaps Father Urbano in San Marco would not be too shocked. He's a reasonable man. But"—she turned back to

Sam—"you mustn't breathe a word of this to anyone else. There'd be a riot."

"A riot, of course. Yes, of course I promise to say nothing. And, Dottoressa, you're right about Father Urbano. He's only a priest, but he reminds me of that great humanist pope, Nicholas the Fifth. Thank you, Dottoressa."

"Lucia."

He murmured it obediently, "Lucia," and stood up to go, teetering a little in his excitement.

She stood up too, and asked a question of her own. "Isn't Signor Kelly a friend of yours?"

"Signor Homer Kelly? Why, yes, he is."

Lucia fell back in her chair. "He wrote me a letter. He tells me he's coming to your conference. But I think"—once again she went off into a gale of laughter—"I think he's another madman. Good-bye, Sam."

※

# CHAPTER 3

*T*he letter with the prospectus had arrived last May in the small house on the shore of Fairhaven Bay in Concord, Massachusetts. Mary Kelly came home from monitoring final exams in Cambridge to find Homer in an ecstasy of excitement.

He had a torn envelope in one hand and its contents in the other. He shouted at her, but his words didn't make sense. They sounded like, "We've got to go to Venice."

"What? Wait, Homer, don't help me. I can take off my own coat."

"I tell you, we can't miss this. Our sabbatical starts next fall. It's the opportunity of a lifetime." Homer pushed Mary into a chair and thrust into her hand the pamphlet from the Biblioteca Marciana.

Dutifully she looked at the impenetrable Italian title.

UN CONVEGNO e UNA MOSTRA INTERNAZIONALE
dall' ETÀ dei MANOSCRITTI all' ETÀ della STAMPA:
I MANOSCRITTI del CARDINALE BESSARIONE
e I LIBRI della TIPOGRAFIA ALDINA

"I'm sorry, Homer, but I've forgotten my Italian."
"Look on the back. It's all in English on the back."
Mary turned the pamphlet over. "Ah, yes, I see."

AN INTERNATIONAL CONGRESS AND EXHIBITION—
THE AGE OF MANUSCRIPTS TO THE AGE OF PRINT:
THE MANUSCRIPT LIBRARY OF CARDINAL BESSARION
AND BOOKS FROM THE ALDINE PRESS

Mary looked up and shook her head. "Cardinal Bessarion? Who's Cardinal Bessarion? I never heard of him."

Homer groaned and lifted his eyes to heaven. "Oh, you poor uneducated farmer's daughter. My dear girl, babies in their bassinets lisp the name of Cardinal Bessarion."

"Oh, come on, Homer, tell me."

"Read what it says. No, I'll read it." Homer snatched the pamphlet and read aloud, "The name of Bessarion evokes for everyone the gift of his great manuscript library to the city of Venice, and his attempt to unite the Greek and Roman churches at the Council of Florence in 1439." He looked up in triumph. "There, you see?"

Mary was still bewildered. Homer looked at her doubtfully. "Well, surely you've heard of the Venetian press of Aldus Manutius?"

"I may have, I'm not sure. But, Homer, what do those people have to do with us? We're students of American literature, not Renaissance scholars."

Homer couldn't believe this display of bovine indifference. He clapped his hand to his forehead and cried, "How could anyone interested in the history of civilization not be moved? How could a woman who professes to tend the dim and flickering light of learning ignore a chance like this? Besides"—Homer calmed down and showed her the letter—"it's from Samuele Bell. He's in charge of the conference and the exhibition. He's the curator of rare books in the Library of Saint Mark in Venice. Cardinal Bessarion's own books were what it began with, way back in the sixteenth century. He's invited us to stay."

"Who, Cardinal Bessarion?"

"No, no, my darling! Samuele Bell! You remember Sam Bell?"

"Oh, yes, of course. He came to Harvard to give the Norton lectures. He speaks English with a delightful accent. Why does he have an English last name?"

"His father was an American but his mother was Italian, so Sam was brought up in Venice. He married a girl from Connecticut, one of those junior-year-abroad kids, but she died a long time ago. He's got a daughter."

"Yes, I remember him now. I liked his jokes." Mary's voice turned dreamy. "He was very attractive."

"Attractive!"

Mary ran into the kitchen, threw open the refrigerator door, and spoke to a bottle of milk, "And of course his lecture was excellent, Homer. I mean, the one I heard. Truly excellent."

"I'll write to say we're coming," said Homer, feverish with anticipation. "We'll have to start organizing. Sam says to bring boots because they sometimes have high water in the fall."

"High water! You mean the city has sunk that far? The Adriatic is beginning to take over?"

"No, no, nothing like that." Homer didn't know what he was talking about, but he flapped his hands carelessly, dismissing the Venetian phenomenon of *acqua alta.* "It's just a few puddles here and there."

"But, Homer, we can't bring our boots, they're so heavy. Are you sure about the puddles?"

Homer was off on another track. "I'll write to Sam at once. And that woman who's just become an important person in the Procuratie Something-or-other. It was in the *New York Times,* big news, I guess, because she's a woman. Lucia somebody. I'll write to her too. I mean, it's a good idea to have—ah—"

"Contacts, Homer?" suggested Mary dryly. "You're making contacts?"

"No, no," said Homer primly, "not *contacts.* Nothing like that at all."

"Oh, well," said Mary resignedly, "we can visit our friends in Florence. And let's hope it's a real sabbatical this time, I mean a real vacation. Let's just pray that for once we don't stumble over any dead bodies. Let's pray you don't have to spend all your time on some idiotic criminal case."

But as it turned out there would be dead bodies aplenty. And yet it was strange—Homer would hardly notice them at all. Tripping over another set of mortal remains he would simply say, "Excuse me," and go blithely on, rejoicing in the study of ancient manuscripts and the blissful deciphering of medieval Latin and Greek.

It was his wife, Mary, who would be left to handle the affair of the dead bodies, who would find herself looking for a collection of missing relics and a lost woman, who would uncover a tragedy half a century old, and bring to light a supremely important vanished work of art.

Homer would be having a lovely, lovely rest.

⅗

And so they came to Venice in October. Their water taxi carried them from the airport on the mainland straight across the lagoon and around the east end of the city to the Riva degli Schiavoni on the south. There in the dazzling light they gaped across the water at a temple rising out of the sea, and disembarked.

Their bags had little wheels. The wheels bumped and zigzagged as Mary and Homer dragged them away from the bright spectacle of the lagoon into a dark passage called Calle del Dose. At once they had to dodge around a black-and-white cat. It was crouched over a plate eating a little silver fish. Then, in exhausted single file, with the rest of their baggage hanging from their shoulders, they made their way across a square. Turning right into the Salizada del Pignater, they passed a little fat girl with a heavy backpack.

She caught up with them as they stood bewildered outside Sam Bell's door. The house bore the correct number in the *sestiere* of Castello, but no one answered Homer's loud knock.

The little girl had a key. Dumbly she inserted it in the lock, opened the door, and looked up at them.

*"Possiamo entrare anche noi, per favore?"* said Mary, who had been working on her Italian.

Without speaking, the child held open the door and they all went in.

*In the Treasury of the Basilica of Saint Mark bronze figures support a rock thrown at Christ during the Flagellation.*

# CHAPTER 4

✂

On this day in early October, Doctor Richard Henchard knew nothing of the arrival in Venice of Mary and Homer Kelly. His entanglement with the Kellys, especially with Mary Kelly, still lay in the future.

Doctor Henchard spoke faultless Italian, although his parents were English. He had been brought up in Plymouth and educated at the University of London, and then he had studied medicine at the ancient University of Bologna and completed his residency in Venice at the Ospedale Civile.

There was a prim Victorian saying, *An Englishman Italianate is a devil incarnate*. It made Henchard laugh. At home in Plymouth he had been humble Rickie Henchard, the son of a butcher. In Venice he was Dottore Primario Richard Henchard, a rich and respected oncological surgeon, and his Italian wife was related to a principessa. Henchard's medical colleagues had trouble with the initial H of his name, and they often called him Riccardo 'Enciard. Even so it was a name to be reckoned with. He was *qualcuno,* a somebody, a person of significance, with or without the H.

As the Kellys walked in the door of Sam Bell's house in the *sestiere* of Castello, Doctor Henchard sat in a realtor's office in Cannaregio. He was looking for an apartment.

"It's for a friend," he told the *agente*. "Cheap. It must be cheap. My friend isn't rich."

Signorina Pastora looked at him shrewdly. He had said *amico,* meaning a male friend, but she strongly suspected his friend was a woman, *un'amica*. She took out her list, thinking with amusement that she wouldn't mind moving into the doctor's little place herself, he was so good-looking.

Her suspicions were correct. Doctor Henchard's friend was a woman, all right, but Giovanna was a tiresome old girl, a pain in the ass, always threatening to call his wife.

"There's a place just around the corner," said Signorina Pastora, getting up. "We'll start with that."

They walked to the Fondamenta dei Mori, across a bridge over the Rio della Sensa. At the moment the canal was a muddy gulf in which a couple of men in rubber boots were shoveling out a channel. "This ugly view is of course only temporary," explained the signorina hastily. "This sort of dredging goes on all the time, as you know, all over the city." Stopping in front of a doorway, she produced a key and added learnedly, "To keep the water moving as a preventive measure against high water."

"Of course," said Henchard, who didn't give a damn what sort of view Giovanna would have.

"Tintoretto lived a few doors down," said Signorina Pastora. "You know, the great painter. Did you see the plaque on the wall?"

Doctor Henchard didn't care about Tintoretto either. He followed her upstairs and watched her unlock another door. "How much?" he said, looking around at the small room.

She named the price. It was extremely low. She explained. "The Nettezza Urbana rents out the space below the apartment for the storage of carts. So the place is cheap. Your friend is lucky. The *spazzini* will not interfere with—him at all. They merely pick up their carts here and push them around the neighborhood to collect everybody's trash."

Henchard made a cursory examination of the bathroom, which was minimal, and glanced at the excuse for a kitchen. "What's that door?"

Signorina Pastora frowned at it. "A closet, I think."

"A closet?" Henchard opened the door and looked at the narrow space within. "Strange."

"True. These old places don't usually have closets."

Henchard ran his hand over the back of the closet, which was lined with wood rather than plaster. One board was loose. As though in disgust, he pulled it off and dropped it to the floor. Turning to Signorina Pastora he said coldly, "My God, this place is in terrible shape. I'll take it for a week on trial."

"Only a week!" Signorina Pastora tried to seem shocked, but she only succeeded in looking tired. The apartment had been without a tenant for a year. If this Casanova wanted a grubby love nest for a week, why should she give a damn? She shrugged. "Well, all right. A week it is."

"The key, please."

She handed it over and said, "Ciao," and thumped down the stairs.

Henchard went to the window and watched her cross the bridge over the empty gulch of the Rio della Sensa. Then he went back into the closet. Bending down, he peered with intense curiosity through the gap in the wooden wall at what lay on the other side.

He had to see more. He tried to rip off another board, but the nails refused to give. He would have to go home for a crowbar.

It took him an hour to go home and come back. Part of the time was spent in explaining to his wife what the crowbar was for. "Rats," he said impulsively. "Doctor Bruno in the office next to mine has rats in the wainscoting. If Bruno has rats today, I'll have them tomorrow."

"Oh, Riccardo, wait," said Vittoria. She ran into the kitchen and came back with a small bottle of dark fluid. "Rat poison. Remember? This is how we took care of it before."

Henchard looked at the bottle with distaste, but he put it in his bag.

As it turned out, it came in handy. When he got back to the house on the Rio della Sensa, he was shocked to discover a real live rat on the premises.

The door to the cart-storage space was wide open. Henchard paused and looked in. He was astonished to see a young man,

obviously one of the *spazzini,* standing up in a big steel cart, using it as a stepladder. His head was out of sight through a hole in the ceiling.

With horror, Henchard understood the geometry at once. The storage space for *carretti* was directly below the little hidden chamber in which he was so feverishly interested.

He walked into the storage room and said softly, "What the *hell* do you think you're doing?"

The legs of the *spazzino* jerked with surprise, and his head came down into view. His hair was white with plaster dust. He coughed and grinned hugely at Henchard. "Ceiling's cracked. A piece fell down." He gestured with a hammer, and said slyly, "I just helped it along a little." His eyes were bright with excitement. "My God, you should see the stuff up there. Gold! All kinds of gold. Hey, wait a minute, look at this!" He reached one arm through the hole, scrabbled around, coughed, and drew his hand out again, holding a large gold plate. He coughed again, and croaked, *"Ecco!"*

Henchard looked at the plate. Slowly he said, "The room up-stairs is private property. It belongs to me."

"It does?" The young man's face fell, and he said, *"Mi dispi-ace."* Coughing, he pushed the plate back up through the hole and stepped down from the cart.

Henchard looked at him soberly. "You have a nasty cough."

"It's just the plaster dust. And you should see all the stuff up there, it's covered with dust." The *spazzino* produced another dry cough.

"Look here," said Henchard, sounding concerned, "I'm a doctor. That cough sounds really serious. It's far down in your lungs. You should take something for it."

"I should?" The young man began coughing in earnest.

If at that moment some wise man had been sitting in a corner of the storage room for carts, looking on with his chin in his hand, some worldly philosopher like the figure of a donor in the painting of a grisly martyrdom, he might have observed that a surgeon's power over life and death could sometimes be too easy.

No philosopher was watching as Henchard opened his bag and took something out. "It just happens that I've got some good stuff right here. You'll have to drink it out of the bottle. It tastes nasty, I'm afraid, but it will do the trick."

It did it very well. The spasms began almost immediately. Henchard laid the boy down on the floor, and said kindly, "I'll call the *ambulanza.*"

The key to the cart-storage space was still in the lock. Hen-chard went outside, shut the door on the boy's groans, turned the key and put it in his pocket. Then he began walking quickly in the direction of the hospital. It wasn't far, and like every other Venetian citizen he was used to walking.

And it gave him time to think. There was a great deal to be done, at once, without delay.

The problem of disposal was one he could handle. After all, he was a surgeon. He knew precisely how to find the point of separation between the patella and the femur. But perhaps there was no point in making careful separations at the joints. He could just go straight across. Of course it would be a messy business, but by the time he came back with his equipment, the blood would not be so apt to spurt all over the place.

And the whole thing could be done right there on the spot. The mess would be no problem. There were ways of dealing with it. And afterward the boy's own colleagues in the employ of the Nettezza Urbana would dispose of the remains. There would have to be a number of plastic bags, but all of the bundles would be quite small. He would simply tie them shut at the top and place them tenderly outside the doors along the *fondamenta,* and in the morning the good workers of the city would pick them up, along with everybody else's plastic bags, and cart them to the nearest canal.

One of the things that had charmed Henchard from his first days in the city was the smoothly working perfection of Venetian civic arrangements. All the problems of life in a watery metropolis had been solved long ago. Since there were no fields, no orchards, no cows or pigs or chickens in this city of stone, everything had to come from the mainland. And of course since there was no extra land anywhere for the disposal of rubbish, every scrap of refuse had to be removed by boat. Henchard had seen rubbish carts hoisted over the seagoing boats of the Netturbini on the edge of the Riva degli Schiavoni, he had seen their bottoms fall open and the debris tumble out. He had seen the fully laden boats chug away into the lagoon.

Out there somewhere, far from the city, they dropped their cargoes. And then, freed of their trash from yesterday—all their smelly garbage and used diapers and tin cans and empty bottles and occasional severed heads and arms and legs—the citizens of Venice could begin the day as fresh and spotless as newborn babes.

Of course the hole in the ceiling would still be a problem. It would call for heavy-gauge chicken wire, a trowel, and a bag or two of plaster of Paris. *Non c'è problema.* Nothing to it.

⌗

# CHAPTER 5

"We are renting the top floor," said Homer to the lit-tle girl, trudging after her up the stairs. "*Siamo qui*—wait a minute—*siamo qui per visitare Dottor Bell. Dov'è*—oh, sorry, hold it a sec." Homer ran over the pos-sessive pronouns in his head. "*Dov' è il suo appartamento?*"

The child seemed not to have heard. She clumped ahead of them, bent nearly double under her backpack. Homer and Mary followed, lugging their baggage up the steps. On the level sur-face of the pavement in the square, the little wheels had made it easy to drag the suitcases, but hoisting them up a flight of stairs was a different matter. Mary and Homer struggled and heaved.

At the first landing the little girl stopped and took out an-other key. Instantly the door was flung open. A woman stood in the doorway and began scolding the child in a torrent of Bosto-nian English. "Ursula, you are a very inconsiderate little girl. Did it occur to you that your grandmother might have some-thing important to do? Where have you been?"

Silently the child edged past her. Only then did the grand-mother notice the man and woman climbing the stairs half a flight down. She stared at them blankly and began to close the door.

"Oh, please, ma'am," said Homer loudly, "perhaps there's some mistake. I spoke to Doctor Bell on the phone yesterday from Concord, Massachusetts."

The woman glowered at them through a crack in the door.

"Oh, Homer," said Mary, embarrassed, "it must be the wrong

address. Can you tell us, signora, if Doctor Samuele Bell lives here?"

At last the face of the grandmother lost its grumpy expression and wreathed itself in smiles. She opened the door all the way. A queenly graciousness replaced the chill. A plump hand was held out in a gesture of royal welcome. "Professor and Mrs. Kelly, of course. Do, *do* come in."

Homer dragged his bag up and up, wanting to say, *It's not Professor and Mrs. Kelly, it's Professor Kelly and Professor Kelly,* but he held his tongue.

"Allow me to introduce myself. I am Dorothea Wellesley. I am an artist. Do come in." But she was still standing in the doorway, a plump elderly woman in a Laura Ashley dress.

*Move out of the way, woman.* Mary and Homer bumped their bags up the last few steps to the landing and stood there, breathing heavily, two exhausted Americans who had just hoisted two hundred pounds of baggage skyward against the downward pull from the center of the earth.

At last Mrs. Wellesley—artist, grandmother, and obviously the mother-in-law of Samuele Bell—stepped aside and they were permitted to enter. At once there was another blockage.

"My art, you see, is here on the wall. This is a portrait of my beloved daughter."

A respectful mortuary pause was required. Mary and Homer supplied it, their book bags dragging from their shoulders, their fists gripping the handles of their suitcases.

"In Venice one can only walk in the footsteps of the masters." Mrs. Wellesley backed up slowly, delivering a lecture on every painting along the corridor. They were apocalyptic scenes in violent colors, the Virgin and child in flames, the crucified Christ in a bonfire, a conflagration of church steeples, a manger scene like a fiery furnace, a robed figure burning at the stake.

Mary inched her bag forward. "Is that the—uh—?"

"The pope? Of course."

Homer was desperate for a bed, a chair, a stretch-out on the floor. He peered past Mrs. Wellesley's livid watercolors at the room beyond the hall. It was a pleasant-looking chamber with cozy chairs and a sofa and delightful puffy pillows. There was a charming sideboard with splendid-looking bottles. Homer recognized one from afar, Old Fence Rail.

He groaned aloud. Mary stepped on his foot, and Homer said, "Ouch," just as the door burst open and Samuele Bell came hurrying in, gasping, shouting a glad greeting.

"I'm sorry to be late. I wanted to be here to welcome you."

Immediately another door opened and the little girl reappeared and ran to her father. He hoisted her with one arm and reached out with the other to shake hands.

"Now, Ursula," said her grandmother severely, "remember your manners."

But the atmosphere was warmer by a dozen degrees. "Sit down, sit down," cried Sam.

Mary and Homer sank into the cozy chairs. Mrs. Wellesley lowered herself daintily into a straight one. Sam plumped himself down on the sofa, bounced his daughter on his knee, and asked urgent questions about their flight from Boston and their state of weariness. Then he set Ursula down and stood up. "You must be perishing for a drink. Speak your poison." He looked around, laughing. "I hope that's right. It's what my father used to say. Something for you, Dorothea?"

"Oh, dear, nothing for me, Sam. Well, perhaps just a smidgen of whiskey."

Homer accepted his Old Fence Rail and laughed with relief, because now at last they had finished their journey. They were at home in this foreign land. He looked around the room, recognizing with pleasure a fellow scholar's quarters. The round table in the middle was littered with books. In the bookcase between the windows other books stood upright, leaned sideways, and lay flat. On the top of the bookcase a bust of Dante looked down at them severely. On the walls, instead of Mrs. Wellesley's frenzied watercolors, there were framed maps of the city of Venice. Originals, decided Homer, and very old. The sailing vessels had high poops, and the puffed cheeks of the four winds blew east, west, north, and south.

Mary jumped up to look at another picture on the wall beside her chair, a green-faced Madonna on a gold background. "Isn't this something pretty wonderful?"

"It's a Paolo Veneziano," said Sam. "There's a bigger one in the Accademia."

"Oh, Sam," said Mrs. Wellesley. "I wish you'd take it down. It's a thoroughly unsuitable subject for a household with a growing child." She tittered. "Worse than pornography, in my opinion."

"Dorothea, you need a drink." Her son-in-law filled her glass. He filled one for Mary too, and she laughed and thanked him, remembering how much she had enjoyed Doctor Bell's way of speaking English with a slight accent when he had been a visiting lecturer in Cambridge. She tried a toast in Italian, probably all wrong. *"Al suo salute!"*

Sam seemed pleased. Mary watched as he pulled the tab on a soft-drink can for his daughter. Then, without making a drink for himself, he sat down again on the sofa and wrapped an arm around the little girl. "Mary and Homer," he said with mock formality, squeezing the child against him, "meet my daughter Ursula. Ursula dear, these two gigantic people are Mr. and Mrs. Kelly from the United States."

Ursula's stony little face opened up. She was beaming.

*In the Treasury of the Basilica of Saint Mark there are many
reliquaries. One contains spines from the Crown of Thorns.*

# C H A P T E R   6

⌖

On the day after the curator of rare books in the Biblioteca Marciana, Dottor Samuele Bell, came into the office of Lucia Costanza and made his outrageous request to examine a number of sacred relics—and an equally outrageous proposal of marriage (it was only a joke, of course)—Lucia descended the stairs from her office and crossed the piazza to consult Father Urbano.

At the east end of the thronged square the Basilica of Saint Mark loomed out of a gray fog like a dream of oriental splendor. In the mist the brilliant colors of the mosaics and the marble columns seemed a little washed out, as though every tourist snapshot had stolen here a blush of rose, there a glitter of gold. On the balustrade above the central portal the bronze horses pawed at the mist, two with the left hoof, two with the right.

There were small pools of water here and there in the square, and a slender stream had seeped into the north aisle of the basilica. Wasn't it early in the year? Lucia splashed through it with her rubber-soled shoes and met Father Urbano in the sacristy.

He was a small round bald-headed priest. When he had been the parish priest of a little village in Umbria he had resembled the Franciscan monks of old, because the shape of his baldness was just like a tonsure.

Father Urbano was not altogether comfortable in the great basilica. Its magnificence sometimes overwhelmed him. In its staring mosaics and golden volumes there was a quality that troubled him, an otherness, as if its builders were not connected to him by blood and bone. They had tossed up over the round

vaults their bulbous domes and designed the great mosaics and attached the tesserae in dazzling clusters, and the mosaics were the wonder of the world, he knew that. And yet their staring eyes disturbed him.

They were indifferent to daily life, to the getting of bread, the raising of children, the doing of laundry. The shimmering figures existed only in eternity, where a peculiar kind of freezing wind had stiffened their limbs and wrinkled their gowns in tortured folds. Their dark brows frowned, their eyes sent long rods of accusation crisscrossing the upper air. It was a web of mighty gazing, never intersecting the upward glances of the tourists shuffling below.

And one of the huge segmented volumes within the basilica aroused in Father Urbano a superstitious dread—for no reason! It was completely absurd! And yet there was something primitive and a little frightening about the hollow cavelike space above the north aisle, as though a shriveled hermit might be squatting in the farthest corner, crouching in a litter of bones, existing on crumbs flown in by pigeons.

Father Urbano had tried to escape his duty. "I don't know, Your Excellency. Perhaps I can be of more service here among my parishioners. Perhaps I'm not *abbastanza sofisticato* for priestly duties in such a famous basilica."

The cardinal patriarch had smiled indulgently. "I disagree, Father. Oh, I know it's beneath your dignity in some ways, keeping track of sinkages and the growth of fungus and the control of crowds and the sale of souvenir booklets. But"—he paused, and Father Urbano knew his cause was lost—"you never can tell when another saint might thrust his arm from a column, and surprise us all." This was a half-irreverent joke, a reminder of the miraculous reappearance of the lost remains of Saint Mark, which had suddenly emerged from a pillar.

But of course there were satisfactions, too, in Father Urbano's unwanted elevation. He had a true vocation for attending to the muttered confessions of every sort of human sin, and a profound and solemn loss of self in the conducting of the mass. And here in Venice he took pleasure in scholarly friendships, enjoying warm exchanges from time to time with the learned scholar Samuele Bell, and with the new procurator of San Marco, Dottoressa Lucia Costanza, who had been a childhood friend.

Today he was amused rather than shocked by her request. *"Andiamo,"* he said, "let's take a look."

A line of tourists was waiting to be admitted to the Treasury of Saint Mark. They looked curiously at the small round priest and the tall woman and murmured resentfully in German, Japanese, and Czech as the ticket seller waved them through. Four of the tourists were from the British Isles. They complained to each other loudly, not caring whether or not they were overheard.

"What right has she got to go to the head of the queue?" said the wife of the bishop of Seven Oaks, far back in the line, craning her neck to stare at Lucia.

"Well, obviously," said the bishop, "that fat little priest likes attractive women."

"Oh, do you think she's attractive?" said his wife, looking at him severely. "Louise, do you think that woman is attractive?"

Louise was the wife of the member of Parliament from the Channel Isles. "Not at all," she said briskly. "Tertius, what do you think? Is that woman attractive?"

"What woman?" said the member of Parliament, who was all at sea.

There were two chambers in the Treasury. One displayed magnificent chalices of blood-red sardonyx from Constantinople, alabaster patens, and amphoras of rock crystal. Lucia had seen these things before. Now she looked at them silently, feeling the solemnity of their antiquity, the aura of their sacred transforming power.

"But this room is beside the point," said Father Urbano. "It's the other one that matters in this case. Come on." They passed the waiting tourists again and walked into the second chamber of treasures. It was filled with reliquaries.

They were new to Lucia. "Tell me about them."

Father Urbano explained. There was no ironic emphasis in

his voice as he led her from one to another. He merely named them quietly, the reliquaries that were like brass sleeves with hands, containing the arm bones of various saints, the bronze chest holding the leg bones of Saint Peter, the small statuettes of brutish men throwing stones at a statuette of Christ.

"Just a minute, Father," said Lucia, staring at the little figures. "That rock on the top—it's real. Is it supposed to be an actual stone from the Flagellation?"

"That's right," said Father Urbano dryly. They moved on and looked at a tooth supported by a cherub. This time he shook his head. "I don't know whose that is."

They stood before a case filled with glass goblets, each with its relic—a small bone or a piece of the True Cross. One held two small needlelike objects. Lucia looked at Father Urbano in disbelief. "They're not—?"

"Yes," said Father Urbano mildly, "they are. Thorns from the Crown of Thorns."

"Thank you, Father," murmured Lucia as they left the Treasury. He unhooked a velvet rope and they sat down in a row of chairs. Lucia found it impossible to hold her tongue. She looked up at the glittering mosaic images above her and said softly, "It would be so easy, so easy."

"I know." Father Urbano sighed. "So easy to pick up a stone and tell a lie, or take a couple of thorns off a bush and tell another lie."

"Or dig up a bone," said Lucia dreamily, "and claim it was something wonderful, when it wasn't at all." She glanced at the procession moving slowly along beside them, waiting to see another wonder, the precious altarpiece called the Pala d'Oro. Then she looked straight ahead at a tall marble column. Was it the one from which the arm of Saint Mark had suddenly appeared, so long ago? "I understand Samuele Bell is a friend of yours. You know, Father, I suppose his examination of the relics might show that some are false, but it might also show"— she turned to him with a direct look—"that some are actually genuine."

Father Urbano smiled and nodded. Lucia suspected that his mind was already made up.

It was. He took her back across the undulating floor of the basilica and led the way into the sacristy. "I'll speak to the cardinal patriarch. He may not agree. But if he does, you understand that there will be requirements, certain restrictions."

"Of course." Lucia thanked him and shook his hand. "If you'll send me the list of requirements, I'll write to Doctor Bell."

&#9763;

The two British couples had "done" San Marco. They had found it a little disappointing, and Tertius Alderney, Conservative member of Parliament for the Channel Isles, was rather alarmed by the puddles in the square.

"I thought you said we didn't have to worry about what's-its-name, high water," he said to Arthur Cluff-Luffter, bishop of Seven Oaks.

"We don't," said the bishop. "This isn't high water. It must have rained in the night, that's all."

"Arthur, it didn't rain," said his wife Elizabeth. "I was awake all night, and there wasn't a drop."

"Oh, dear," said Louise Alderney, "why didn't somebody tell me to bring my wellies?"

# CHAPTER 7

W hen the list came to her office in a formal letter of permission from the cardinal patriarch, Lucia was sitting at her desk composing another letter.

It was a painful letter, one she had been rehearsing in her mind for months. The time had come at last. The insults were too grievous. It wasn't just other women, although that was tiresome enough. It was her husband's pathetic posturing, his refusal to take a job unworthy of his sensitive nature, his bitter explosions of childish rage because she was so good a provider. Even so, it took three drafts before Lucia could control her anger and write something clear and sensible.

Lorenzo,
I'm leaving you. You know why. I'm taking an apartment. I've withdrawn all my savings from the bank. Enclosed is a certified check for half the entire sum.

L

As soon as she had inserted the check and the letter in an envelope, sealed the envelope, addressed it to her husband, stamped it with a thump of her fist, and dropped it on the pile of outgoing mail, Lucia wrote the next letter with more pleasure.

Of course she could have run downstairs and hurried around the corner and entered the library and related her good news in person, but in a controversial matter of this kind she must preserve all the dry ceremony of official business.

Her second letter was addressed to—

*Dottor Samuele Bell*
*Biblioteca Marciana*
*San Marco 7*
*30124 Venezia*

⊠

*T*he place wasn't very good, but it would be all right for now. It could probably be fixed up. The kitchen needed new appliances and a coat of paint. Of course the hole in the wall of the closet would have to be repaired right away. It was amazing how flimsy these old places were. The connecting wall was disintegrating, falling apart at a touch.

The space on the other side surely belonged to the people next door. It must be part of their house, not this one. It looked like a storage room for their castoffs—beautiful castoffs, really remarkable—but they were no business of this tenant. Perhaps Signorina Pastora at the agency would speak to the other people about repairing the wall.

⊠

Doctor Richard Henchard sat again in the client's chair in the office of the realtor from whom he had rented the dingy apartment on the Rio della Sensa. "I'll take it for another six weeks," he said grandly.

"Oh, I'm sorry, but it's been rented to someone else for a year." Signorina Pastora frowned. "You said you wanted it for only a week."

"What?" Henchard stared at her in horror. "You mean you showed it to someone else while I was out?"

"No, as a matter of fact I didn't." She was on the defensive. "I loaned this person a key and said take a look for yourself, only knock first, so the client went over there and decided to take it and came back and signed a lease and gave me a month's rent."

Henchard stood up from his chair and leaned over her desk. "I'll take it for a year. I'll give you a year's rent. Now, right now."

Signorina Pastora was surprised into telling the truth. "But why? The place isn't worth it."

Henchard slapped his checkbook down on the desk and looked at her.

"Oh well, all right." She shook her head as if reluctant. "I'll have to tell the other party that I got the papers mixed up, and you already had a lease. But—" She laughed, and watched him scribble the check. God, he was attractive.

Thrusting it at her, he said, "Who was it? Tell me. What's his name?"

The phone rang. "Excuse me." Signorina Pastora talked and listened and talked, radiating charm. "Oh, yes, signor, there are many delightful properties, but of course they're all very expensive. Yes, of course I'll be happy to show you one or two. Yes, certainly, I'm free this afternoon. I'll meet you by the monument to Goldoni at two. Oh, don't you know it? Let me explain." It was another two minutes before she put down the phone, while Henchard controlled his rage. At last she looked up at him and said, "I'm sorry, what was your question?"

"His name! What is the name of the person who wanted to rent that apartment for a year?"

"Oh, I can't tell you that. These things are strictly confidential." The phone rang again. "I'm sorry, excuse me."

The call was apparently intimate. She swung around in her revolving chair and faced away from Henchard and whispered into the phone.

Delicately he reached for the papers on her desk and fingered them silently until he found the name he wanted, complete with the address. The handwriting was strong and distinctive, the hand of somebody of importance like himself. Probably he too wanted a place for his girlfriend.

When Signorina Pastora swung around again to face Henchard, the papers were back where they belonged.

"Anything else?"

Then he remembered that Giovanna still needed an apartment. The idiot kept whimpering and complaining, insisting that if she didn't have something better than the cathouse she'd move in with his wife. "Yes," said Henchard, "as a matter of fact, there is. I need another apartment. Cheap, really cheap."

By the time he had made an appointment to see another rental it was late. He was in a panic. What if the man to whom Signorina Pastora had loaned a key had opened the closet door of the apartment while inspecting the place? What if he had seen the opening at the back? What if he had looked through the gap and seen what was hidden behind it? Jesus Christ!

Henchard plunged across the bridge over the Rio della Sensa, which was still a muddy crevasse, and turned right at the figure of the Moor on the corner of the Campo dei Mori. Swiftly he bounded past the Casa del Tintoretto and the three neighboring houses.

Then he floundered to a stop. A woman was coming out of the apartment door. She was well dressed, and handsome in a statuesque kind of way.

He gaped at her, and babbled, "*Mi dispiace, signora,* but this is my house."

She looked at him kindly. "You are mistaken." She nodded at the next house. "Perhaps you have the wrong door."

Ah, of course, it was the girlfriend! Her distinguished boyfriend didn't know yet about the realtor's change of mind. "I'm sorry, signora, it's the agency's mistake. Signorina Pastora is a little"—Henchard twirled a finger at his forehead—"muddled. She rented the place twice. I'm sorry to tell you this, but my lease is earlier than yours." He pulled it out of the inner pocket of his jacket, passed it swiftly under the woman's eyes, and put it back. "Tell your—ah—friend to call her. She will confirm what I say."

"My friend?" The woman looked puzzled.

"May I have your key?"

She looked bewildered for a moment, and then agreed. "Well, all right, never mind." Fumbling in her bag, she produced a key and turned away.

He gazed at her back. For a whore she was in a class by herself, not at all like simpleminded Giovanna. Henchard was enormously relieved that she wasn't making a fuss, that she had handed him her key so willingly. It meant she didn't know what she was giving up. But of course her boyfriend might know, the fool who thought he had rented the apartment.

Gasping, Henchard ran up the stairs, unlocked the apartment door, and burst into the room.

To his dismay he saw that the closet door was open a few inches, and when he flung it wide he saw to his horror that another board had fallen to the floor. The narrow slit between the remaining boards was now twelve inches wide. The fucking bastard had put his eye to the hole and seen Henchard's priceless treasure. Shit!

But now, Christ, he had to get back to the office. There were patients to see, a grim phone call to make.

After that it was perfectly plain what had to be done, and done without delay.

# CHAPTER 9

✄

The great conference had not yet begun, although a few scholars from here and there were already nosing around the Biblioteca Marciana, getting in the way, having to be rescued from the fierce clutches of the official dragon at the door with her insistence on some reason why they should be admitted, people of the exalted stature of the Herr-Direktor of the Kunst Historisches Museum in Vienna, two scholars from the Uffizi, two more from the Morgan Library in New York, and the curator of early printed books in Chicago's Newberry Library.

These august visitors kept turning up, much too soon, while preparations were still frantically in progress. There they would be, eminently important people cooling their heels in the entry of the Marciana under the dark suspicious gaze of the dragon until Sam could be summoned. And then he would have to come downstairs to apologize in person, and spend the rest of the day taking them to lunch and showing them around, and explaining about the water slipping over the stone banks of the canals at certain times of day.

"Oh, no matter," exclaimed the man from the Houghton Library at Harvard. "After all, I spend half my time in swamps, studying the flora and fauna."

"And surely this is nothing!" said the woman from the British Museum. "I was expecting Noah's Flood!"

"Should we start pairing off?" joked the director of the Fitzwilliam. "Two camels, two giraffes, two students of early

printed books?" He winked at the woman from the British Museum, but she pursed her mouth.

And therefore Sam was harried and worried, but Homer Kelly basked in happiness. He adored libraries, any library, from a closet full of books in a rural town hall to the vast collections of Widener Library in Harvard Yard. To Homer, libraries were holy places like churches, and the priestly librarians a blessed race, a saving remnant in a world of sin. Whenever God grew impatient and decided to destroy the world he remembered the librarians and stayed his hand. At least that was Homer's opinion. This library too was holy ground.

And he was helping! Sam had drafted Homer to fetch and carry. He was permitted to enter the sacred storage vault and extract one priceless volume after another and carry it up through a private passage into the magnificent reading room, the Sala della Libreria.

This reading room was not like the workaday one downstairs, marvelous as that chamber might be. It was a masterpiece of the Venetian High Renaissance, every inch of it decorated by Venetian artists and craftsmen. Here, surrounded by glory upon glory, Homer Kelly and Sam's other assistants unwrapped the beautiful volumes from the bubble envelopes that protected them against woodworm.

With reverent hands Homer helped place them upright in the display cases. Then Sam Bell himself walked up and down, choosing the pages to be held open with satin ribbons.

When the work was done, Homer spent an hour ogling the elegant pages, trying to read the Latin names. He could guess at Sallust's *Catiline*, which was adorned with floating cherubs, but Sam had to help him with the Greek titles, Ptolemy's *Geography* and the Epistles of Paul.

"How many books did Cardinal Bessarion have altogether?" said Homer, gazing at the foliated initials of a Latin Livy.

"Oh, thousands. That's why the library had to be built to house them." Sam took Homer's arm and led him to a case across the aisle. Leaning over it, he breathed a reverent mist on the glass. "Of course you're aware, Homer, that the printing press of Aldus Manutius was one of the first in Venice. This is his masterpiece, *The Dream of Poliphilius*. I think it's the most beautiful book ever printed."

Homer was six feet six inches tall, his beard was gray and bushy, and he was fifty years old, but he wanted to weep like a child. His wife Mary sometimes complained about the way he was forever being hooked by some new obsession. The man was incapable of being bored by anything human, nor by any branch of learning, no matter how feeble his understanding. Now he was overwhelmed with sentimental awe, and he made a gulping sound in his throat.

Sam clapped him on the back. "Come on. *Facciamo uno spuntino*. I've got a bottle of Prosecco in my office. I'll just make sure there aren't any dignitaries with hurt feelings swarming around downstairs."

They walked through the glorious vestibule, where Homer craned his neck to admire Titian's allegorical figure of Wisdom on the ceiling—obviously a library enthusiast herself because she was consulting both a book and a scroll. Then they descended

Sansovino's stupendous staircase, negotiated the open-air arcade, and walked up another set of stairs. As they climbed the second long flight very slowly—Sam was tired and Homer was out of shape—Sam told himself once again that nothing mattered anymore. He could do whatever he wanted.

He could abandon everything, the whole damn thing, the exhibition and the conference and all his duties as caretaker of some of the most valuable books in the Western world. He could flee from all of that and embark in a little boat with Dottoressa Lucia Costanza, and its pink sail would be blown by a gentle wind, carrying them to the island of Cythera. It would be so easy, so simple. All he had to do was entice her away from the eminence of her procuratorship, burst her marriage chains, and make love to her at last in some flowery bower.

"What did you say, Homer? Oh, of course, here we are. Come right in."

The telephone was ringing in the outer office. Sam's secretary held up the phone and murmured, *"Il sindaco."*

"The mayor," said Sam apologetically, waving Homer on into the big room with its view of the lagoon. When he hurried in a few minutes later, he explained that the mayor was organizing a council to deal with *acqua alta.* "You know, consisting of everybody around the piazza."

*"Acqua alta?"* said Homer. "Oh, you mean high water. Right. Well, it's here already. It's not so bad."

Sam looked at him in disbelief. "Just wait, Homer," he said. "You haven't seen anything yet."

"Nothin'," said Homer, correcting Sam's English. "I ain't seen nothin' yet."

Sam looked puzzled. "But isn't that bad grammar?"

"You betcha," said Homer, grinning at him.

"Ah, a colloquial expression," said Sam. He poured bubbly wine into Homer's glass, lifted his own, and then, to show that he too was acquainted with American slang, he said, "Well, here's dirt in your eye."

Homer let it pass, and went back to the subject of the great cardinal. "Tell me, Sam, has the library got every single one of Bessarion's books?"

"Oh, no. A great many are missing. The library didn't exist until long after he gave them to the city. So they were stored in crates here and there, and borrowed like library books, so some fell by the wayside. And then that blundering idiot Napoleon Bonaparte decided to found an Italian library, so a lot of Bessarion books sat around in Padua, waiting for it, only it never happened, and they began to disappear. That's what I've heard."

"But what about the printed books? Are there any more of that divine *Dream of Poliphilius* still kicking around somewhere?"

"Oh, yes, a few. They're outrageously valuable."

Homer leaned back in his chair and looked at the row of portraits on the wall over Sam Bell's head. "Who are all those people? Your predecessors, I'll bet. Will your picture be up there someday, the distinguished *conservatore dei libri rari,* Dottor Samuele Bell?"

Sam winced. He glanced up at the painted series of scholar-professors. He had known some of them in person. Not one of those dignified people, so far as he knew, had ever dreamed of abandoning his duties and embarking with a lady love for the fanciful island of Cythera, that blessed place sacred to Venus, where lovemaking lasted into eternity, and where there was no death.

✄

The phone was ringing. Ursula picked it up and said a timid *"Pronto?"*

A strong male voice asked for Dottor Samuele Bell, but at once her father picked up the phone in his study.

Instead of hanging up, Ursula listened.

When they were finished she went silently into her room and closed the door. After a while she came out again and checked to see if her grandmother had come home from shopping.

No, she hadn't. Ursula hurried straight into her grandmother's bedroom and opened the drawer where Mrs. Wellesley kept pills, bottles of perfume, violet and green eye shadow, black mascara, false eyelashes, wrinkle-control creams, and a messy jewel box spilling over with bracelets, brooches, button earrings, old pairs of bifocals, and strings of cultured pearls.

There was an envelope under the jewel box. Ursula extracted it and helped herself to a five-thousand-lire note. Then she tucked the envelope back where it belonged, closed the drawer gently, and slipped out of the room.

Next day after school, she stopped in the shop.

*"Buonasera, piccola,"* said the man behind the counter. *"Un altro, oggi?"* You must have quite a collection by now. Which one would you like today?"

"That one, please," said Ursula.

# C H A P T E R   1 1

⚙

M ary had been having a good time too. She had been going out every day to explore the city, not minding that the camera around her neck made her look like a tourist. After all, she *was* a tourist, an eager inquisitive tourist who consulted her guidebook at every street corner and struggled to unfold and fold her map while the wind blew its creases the wrong way.

Before leaving Massachusetts she had bought ten rolls of film at a discount pharmacy. Now she had begun using them freely. Her camera was always at the ready. *When in doubt, push the button.* She didn't care how trite her subjects were, or how many other tourists were taking the same pictures. She envisioned the mills of Kodak grinding out enormous batches of identical shots of the same famous places. She didn't care.

At first Mary had a plan. She would explore one part of the city at a time and keep a list of every picture she took. On the first day she had been scrupulous about recording every shot:

1. Riva degli Schiavoni, statue of Vittorio Emanuele
2. View of the lagoon with San Giorgio Maggiore
3. Another view of the lagoon
4. Gondolas carrying Japanese tourists under the Bridge of Sighs

Tour groups from Japan were everywhere. Mary imagined a travel agent in Tokyo offering dirt-cheap package tours. In Venice the Japanese were polite and interested, but they had

come in such numbers that they sometimes blocked her way. Courteously they squeezed together as they stopped to take pictures. They were obviously as eager as she was to record the fabulous city and keep it forever. She couldn't avoid capturing them in the foreground of her pictures of Santa Maria della Salute and the Rialto Bridge. And of course many of their multitudinous shots would show one Mary Kelly as a miscellaneous object in front of the clock tower in Piazza San Marco, a woman striding past the Campanile or moving among the pigeons in the square.

Whether they wanted to or not, they were capturing each other's faces. Next month in Tokyo the tall solid figure of an American woman would appear on screens in a hundred darkened rooms. She would be an anonymous part of the background behind beaming rows of family members. And her own Venetian scrapbook would show flocks of Japanese visitors feeding the pigeons, admiring the four bronze horses over the portals of San Marco, or sitting at the little tables in front of Florian's.

Today the two British couples were in everybody's pictures too, having lunch at Florian's, sitting under the arcade eating fish soup and drinking white wine while the man at the piano played Broadway show tunes.

"There's a striking-looking woman," said the bishop, taking off his reading glasses and staring across the square at Mary Kelly.

"Where?" said his wife, turning her head through an angle of one hundred and eighty degrees.

The wife of the member of Parliament glanced over her shoulder and shrugged. "American, I think."

*"Porto ora il secondo piatto?"* said the waiter. "If you please, the second course?"

*"Mi piace spaghetti alle vongole,"* said the bishop at once, showing off, getting the reflexive pronoun right, forgetting that *spaghetti* was a plural noun.

His wife ordered *fegato alla veneziana,* then let the rest of them in on a secret. She was beginning a novel set in Venice, full of rotting palaces, crumbling bridges, stinking canals, and leering gondoliers. "Honestly, it's all in my head. All I have to do is put pen to paper, so to speak."

The piano player ran his finger up the keyboard and splashed into "Younger Than Springtime," and Mary Kelly moved out of sight into the Piazzetta and took a picture of the Ducal Palace.

*When in doubt push the button. More is better. Push the button, push the button, change the film, push the button.*

# CHAPTER 12

✄

Doctor Richard Henchard wandered around the room for a few minutes, thinking quickly, his eyes darting here and there. Then to quiet his beating heart he sat down in a comfortable chair beside the body of Lorenzo Costanza, and read once again the letter from Costanza's wife that he had found on the table—

Lorenzo,
    I'm leaving you. You know why. I'm taking an apartment. I've withdrawn all my savings from the bank. Enclosed is a certified check for half the entire sum.

                                                                    L

Henchard couldn't help grinning. *You know why.* Well, of course the poor *sciocco* knew why. Henchard knew why too. The man had a wandering eye. He'd rented that place on Rio della Sensa, or tried to rent it, for the same reason Henchard himself had taken it, for a girlfriend. The man who now lay dead on the floor had wanted a place for the handsome woman Henchard had met coming out of the apartment.

So naturally he had never told his wife about it. It wasn't the sort of thing you told your wife. Costanza's wife was probably another fat bitch just like Vittoria, his own wife. She wasn't in on her husband's little secrets. She knew nothing about the apartment and its contents. She guessed that he was two-timing her, that was all. Wives, they always knew.

Well, the poor bastard had lost his wife and his life on the same day. But he had also, thank God, lost the treasure that lay behind the closet wall in the house on Rio della Sensa.

The letter looked useful somehow. What could he do with it? Lovingly Henchard fingered the check, but he couldn't possibly cash it. That would be madness.

Getting up, he began exploring the rest of the house. It was a handsome place, tastefully furnished with country cupboards and Biedermeier chairs. In Signora Costanza's bedroom he rummaged in the bureau drawers. And there, to his flabbergasted delight, he found among the underwear—*eccolo!*—a handgun of precisely the same make and model as his own. *"Un modello molto popolare,"* the dealer in the Milanese gunshop had told him. *"Anche io, ho la stessa pistola."* The dealer had the same gun himself!

It lay there like a miracle among the brassieres and panties. Surely the woman had handled it—her prints must be all over it. Reverently he picked it up with a pair of the silken panties and wondered how to make use of this stroke of luck. What if he were to make this man's death look like a suicide? It was wonderful what you could learn from television—you just squeezed the dead fingers around the grip of the gun, and there you were.

But did he actually *want* a suicide? What if he made it look as if the man's own wife had killed him?

The more he thought about it, the better he liked it. The gun already bore the wife's fingerprints. He would take away his own identical piece, the one that had actually done the deed, and leave hers in its place, a weapon of the same caliber using the same cartridges, covered all over with her own prints. What's more—Henchard laughed out loud—she had run away! It would look highly suspicious. And what about her bank account! She had withdrawn all the money from her bank account! Better and better!

Carrying the signora's gun still safely wrapped in her panties, Henchard went back downstairs. Stepping over the body of Lorenzo Costanza, he went to the window and peered out, looking for a place to deposit the weapon. It had to be just right. It mustn't be so well hidden that it would not be found immediately, but on the other hand it mustn't seem planted on purpose. It should look as though the woman in her emotional distress and in a fever of guilty remorse had tossed it away and fled.

All the houses along this pleasant street in the *sestiere* of San Polo had little front gardens. This one was just right. Henchard opened the window softly and dropped the woman's weapon into the ground cover below.

Closing the window, he wondered what else he could do to incriminate the lady. Her departure must look like a hasty retreat. He went upstairs again to her bedroom and examined the wardrobe. It was nearly empty. Obviously she had already taken away most of her clothes.

Artfully Henchard took a few pieces of her leftover underwear from the drawer in which he had found the weapon, threw them on the bed, and scattered more on the floor.

He was almost ready to go. There was only one thing more.

In the kitchen he found a box of matches. Henchard scratched a match against the side of the box and held the flame under the envelope that contained the certified check and Lucia's farewell note. It flared up. When it was nearly consumed, he dropped it in the sink, blew on his scorched fingers, and washed the ashes down the drain.

Before leaving the house he went back to the room where the body lay. In his surgical practice Henchard had seen many anesthetized men and women, and all of them had shown this same helpless look. They had been transformed from lively, upright, intelligent beings into logs of wood. If they were Henchard's patients they woke up and resumed their active selves, at least for a while—obviously some were doomed. But this log of wood was stone dead. It would never rise again.

In the city of Plymouth, where Henchard had been raised, his mother had been a member of the Plymouth Brethren, and always there had been a heavy emphasis on the necessity to separate oneself from evil, to avoid every possible contact with sin. Of course young Ricky had paid no attention to his mother, but

he couldn't help remembering some of her sour maxims and
guilt-inducing platitudes—*This have I done for thee. What hast
thou done for me?*

Later on, at the time of his marriage in Venice, he had been
baptized a Roman Catholic, and another weight of moral re-
proof had landed on his shoulders.

Both of these influences had been feeble, and he had
shrugged them off. Yet now as he looked at the dead man they
peered around the corner of his conscience.

Today in the operating room of the Ospedale with a gastric
carcinoma under his knife, something else had affected him.
Poised over the tumor he had seen a sharp vision of the an-
guished face of the dying *spazzino,* and it had given him a turn.
"Separate thyself from evil," cautioned his mother. "Repent and
thy sins will be forgiven," promised the Holy Father.

As Henchard made his escape from the house of Lucia and
Lorenzo Costanza, he added another item to his list of the things
to be done next day. Between a colon resection and a lumpec-
tomy he would stop off in San Marco and make a proper papist
confession. He would whisper to the priest behind the curtain,
*Father, I have sinned,* and the priest would tell him to go in
peace and say a hundred Hail Marys. Or should he confess to a
mortal sin? *Father, I have committed a mortal sin.* Henchard's
wife was always talking about mortal sin. Adultery, she said, was
a mortal sin.

It didn't matter, one way or the other. He would make his
confession to that famous priest in San Marco, and then there
would be no more painful visions.

✠

*T*he official letter to Samuele Bell from Lucia Costanza arrived only three days after Sam's visit to her office. On
that day he had come away besotted, but of course there
were overwhelming reasons why he could not pursue the matter,
namely—

Reason One
and
Reason Two.

The letter was strictly formal:

Dottor Samuele Bell
Biblioteca Marciana
San Marco 7
30124 Venezia

Gentilissimo Dottor Bell,
    Enclosed is a copy of a letter I have sent to His Excel-
lency, Pietro Caravello, Cardinal Patriarch of the Basilica
of San Marco. As you see, it is a formal request for his co-
operation in your study of the authenticity of the relics in
the Treasury.
    Also included is his official response, agreeing to the
project under very specific terms, which are as follows:
    For every loan there will be documents requiring your
signature. No more than fifteen objects at a time may be

borrowed from the Treasury. Transport will require the presence of one carabiniere, both going and coming. Each object may remain in your possession for only thirty days.

The only slightly personal note in the letter was a final warning—

As the caretaker of precious volumes in the Marciana you will understand the necessity of absolute promptness in the return of every relic. None may be kept out "overdue."

Distinti saluti

Dottoressa Lucia Costanza,
Procuratore di San Marco

Sam was overjoyed. He sat at his desk savoring the letter and its enclosures, delighted not only with the opportunity for debunking superstition, but also with the fact that he now had a reason for speaking to the dottoressa again.

He called her office at once.

*"Pronto?"* The voice was loud and masculine.

"This is Dottor Samuele Bell. May I speak with Dottoressa Costanza?"

There was a slight pause. "Perhaps you have not read the paper," said Lucia's assistant, whose name, Sam remembered, was Bernardi.

"The paper! No! What's happened?"

"Signora Costanza's husband has been murdered, and the signora is missing."

"What!"

"And I regret to say," continued Bernardi mercilessly, "an object from her desk is missing as well, a certain very precious statuette." Bernardi fingered the heavy lump in the pocket of his trousers. The statuette was a seventeenth-century bronze centaur, as valuable as it was charming.

Sam tried to speak, but Bernardi interrupted. "In her absence I am acting as procurator, although my permanent appointment

will of course be delayed. And I must say, Signor Bell, on review-
ing her recent letter to you concerning various sacred relics, I
think Signora Costanza's rash decision must be reconsidered."

"*Dottoressa* Costanza," said Sam sharply, almost beside himself, "she is a dottoressa," and he slammed down the phone.

It was a little while before he could recover himself enough to
go out for a paper. And then when he stumbled down two
flights of stairs to the entry hall, he saw out of the corner of his
eye the imposing figure of a museum director from Hong Kong.
The man was darting forward to cut him off.

Sam grinned at him with all his teeth and made a clumsy dash
for the door. Outside in the arcade he almost collided with a gigantic African scholar in a green robe, gold sandals, and white
socks. *"Mi dispiace,"* cried Sam in apology, and hurried away
around the corner.

The Molo was thick with tourists. He moved against the tide,
heading for the newsstand at the vaporetto stop, where one of
the vaporetti was just pulling up, grinding against the floating
dock. Tourists poured out and moved eagerly toward the Pi-
azetta as Sam paid for two local papers and unfolded the first
with nervous fingers.

Oh, God, yes, there was the story on the front page of *Il
Gazzettino*—

*PROCURATORE COSTANZA UN' OMICIDA?*

Below the brutal headline was a dim photograph of the murdered husband, *Signor Lorenzo Costanza*.

Sam fumbled his way across the moving crowd of jolly
tourists, jolly couples taking pictures of each other, jolly mamas
pushing jolly baby buggies, and sat down on the stone wall at
the edge of the water. *Gondole, gondole,* sang out a jolly gondolier in a striped shirt, drumming up trade. The gondolas lay
rocking below the barrier, their brass fittings glinting joyfully in
the sun.

The writer of the article seemed to regard himself as *un giornalista investigativo*. With obvious delight he listed the sordid elements of the story:

1. The murdered husband
2. The vanished wife, *una donna eminente*
3. The discovery in the bushes of a handgun with the wife's fingerprints
4. The apparent haste of her departure
5. The *previous* removal of her entire savings from the Cassa di Risparmio di Venezia

Sam understood at once the heavy implication of the word *previous*. The violent act must have been premeditated.

The story was continued on page 3. Sam's fingers couldn't find page 3. They kept turning to page 5, with its forecast of extremely high water in Venice in November, or to the report on page 7 from Padua, where fifteen thousand turkeys had been asphyxiated overnight.

At last his fingers trembled open the right page, and there at the bottom was another article, an interview with a woman who had been Lucia's neighbor in the *sestiere* of San Polo. It was headed LA VECCHIA STORIA. Sam read it with disgust.

*It was the old, old story* (tearfully reported Signora Adelberti). *SHE was ambitious, HE was a man with a poetic nature. The dottoressa was too busy with her important career to nurture him in his loneliness, to comfort him in his sad state of unemployment, and thus he was forced into the arms of others.*

With gravely careful fingers Sam refolded his *Gazzettino* and walked back to work. He did not examine the rest of the paper. He failed to see the item on page 16, a tiny paragraph with the modest heading *Spazzino Smarrito*.

The fact that a young trash collector employed by the Nettezza Urbana had disappeared, as well as the distinguished woman who was a newly appointed procurator of San Marco, rang no bells in Sam's mind at all.

## CHAPTER 14

✂

*T*he confessional in the north aisle of the Basilica of San Marco was a magnificent piece of baroque woodcarving, but behind the rosy curtain the space was as dark and intimate as if it were an ordinary clumsy box in a country church. Father Urbano's comfortable bulk nearly filled it.

Today he had his ear against the curtain, but still he could barely hear the hoarse whispering of the man kneeling outside. Perhaps it was the accent that obscured his words. Was he British perhaps? Or American? He was confessing an unspecified mortal sin, yet at the same time he seemed to expect automatic absolution. It was apparent that he did not understand the sacrament of confession at all.

"My son, you must name your sin."

"Name my sin! For Christ's sake, Father, just tell me my penance."

Father Urbano looked up over the red curtain of the confessional to the golden dome of the Pentecost. All the apostles sat around it in a ring with tongues of fire descending on their heads. The mighty wind that rushed upon them from heaven had not rumpled a single robe nor tossed a single strand of apostolic whisker, but every one of them now possessed the gift of speaking in tongues.

For a moment Father Urbano's own tongue was tied. Then he spoke in his usual way about the certainty of God's mercy and God's love, and cautioned that there could be no penance nor absolution until the sin was told. "My son," he said again, "you must name your sin."

In reply there was a long silence. At last Father Urbano parted the curtain and looked out. The man was gone. But someone else had taken his place. A child was looking up at him expectantly.

"My dear," said Father Urbano, "what do you want?"

She said nothing, but she got down on her fat little knees, as if in imitation of the man who had just hurried away.

"Little one," said Father Urbano, "you are very young. Have you been prepared for your first confession?"

She shook her head. Then a woman appeared suddenly, snatched the child's hand, pulled her to her feet, and scolded her in English. "Ursula, what on *earth* do you think you're doing?" With a baleful glance at Father Urbano she rushed the little girl away.

He was left standing in the aisle, feeling at a loss. He should have helped, he should have said something encouraging. The poor child, somehow he had failed her.

✄

M ary got up early and prepared for another day of exploration. She stuck her folding umbrella in her bag along with her guidebook, her pocket dictionary, a sandwich, and a mirror and comb. Tucked into her billfold were her Venetian phone card, a slip entitling her to one more visit to the toilet near San Marco, and her *abbonamento,* the ticket that allowed her freedom of travel on the Grand Canal, anywhere, any time, by vaporetto.

First stop, the Accademia, because Venice was a city of painters. Here Mary would find them all assembled—the three Bellinis, Carpaccio, Giorgione, Titian, Tintoretto, Tiepolo, Veronese, Lotto, Guardi, Canaletto! There was no end to the supply of great Venetian painters. They had set each other off, one skyrocket igniting another.

But when she stepped down from the vaporetto, she was too early for the Accademia. It would not open for hours. Listlessly she bought a paper at the kiosk and sat down on a bench. Newspaper Italian was easy to guess at. There was a murder on the front page, but it meant nothing to Mary Kelly. Gloomily she tossed the paper in a trash basket, and looked mournfully at the palaces across the Grand Canal.

Church bells were bonging. From somewhere came the piping bark of a dog. A gull floated in and out of the sunlight. She was homesick.

Oh, it was so stupid. Here she was in this most ravishing of all cities, and yet she was languishing for her own kitchen back home, her own daily round, her own view of Fairhaven Bay, her own car, her own free life, her own cozy office in the Yard. She longed to find herself in the library in Concord, looking up at the familiar busts of Bronson Alcott and Ebenezer Rockwood Hoar. She hungered for the morning news on the radio. She was ashamed to admit even to herself that she missed watching her favorite television programs, propped up on pillows beside Homer in their comfortable bed.

It was just a momentary silliness. Mary had been through it before. It was merely the heavy imprinting of habit on body and brain. She remembered a scornful joke of Emerson's about the poor blockheads in Paris who had to do the best they could, even though they had never seen Bateman's Pond or Nine Acre Corner or Becky Stow's swamp.

Homesickness was the worst kind of provincial chauvinism. *What, all you've got are a hundred magnificent churches and a thousand painted masterpieces and scores of pretty bridges and a fleet of charming gondolas on canals the color of jade? Where are your muskrats? Where's your purple loosestrife? Where's Vander-Hoof's Hardware Store?*

It would pass. Mary knew it would pass. The delight in this extraordinary place would return. It was like being seasick for a few days on a ship.

The vaporetto was coming. It was a lumbering water-bus, churning up to the Accademia stop and crashing into the floating dock. She waited with the others for the passengers to disembark, then hurried aboard, slid open the door to the seating compartment, and found a place beside a window.

Sitting with her canvas bag between her knees, she extracted her map of the city and decided to get off at the Rialto and follow her nose, obeying her maxim to take pictures of everything. *Push the button, push the button.*

In the meantime there was the whole panorama of the Grand Canal to gawk at, with its changing parade of palaces. Mary glanced back and forth between her map and the view, and held her camera up to the window, taking pictures of one palace after another—Loredan, Rezzonico, Foscari, Papadopoli. Then she

transferred her attention to the lively craft on the water—the vaporetti going and coming and the working boats bringing everything necessary for life from the mainland. One carried bottles
of *acqua minerale gassata,* another a load of plastic chairs. The
men at the tillers hailed each other and raised clenched fists in
greeting. *Quick, push the button.* Then she turned her camera
lens on a floating pile driver that was smashing thick poles into
the water with heavy hammer blows. A red speedboat of the
Vigili del Fuoco came along, throwing up a bow wave, and then
a blue one of the polizia, roaring by in the other direction.

But it was the gondolas that were the most delectable subjects, as though they had survived from ages past merely to have
their pictures taken. Mary could see that they were no good as
transporters of human cargo from place to place, certainly not in
competition with this clumsy water-bus. You didn't hire a gondola to get somewhere. It was strictly an aesthetic experience.

They were irresistible. Mary took picture after picture through
the window of the vaporetto, trying to capture the grace of the
gondoliers as they stood in the stern, shifting gently from one
foot to the other, rocking slightly forward and back.

She was almost too late to get off at her stop. The Rialto
Bridge loomed up before she was ready. The vaporetto was already scraping the floating dock.

Mary jumped out of her seat and crowded forward, just managing to get off before the next crowd of passengers surged on
board. The floating dock swiveled and rocked. Mary staggered
and collided with a dignified-looking man. *"O, mi dispiace, signore,"* she gasped, recovering her balance.

*What news on the Rialto?* That was from *The Merchant of
Venice.* And it was what Henry Thoreau had called the Milldam,
"Concord's Rialto," where the old men sat gossiping outside the
shops, where Henry had to run the gauntlet. The word meant
*busy,* it meant *commercial,* it meant this bustle of people going
and coming. It meant cries of *Gondole, gondole* from gondoliers
in straw hats, it meant tourists dragging baggage up the long as-
cent of the bridge, it meant places for cashing traveler's checks,

it meant scarves and fanciful carnival masks for sale, and kiosks selling postcards and T-shirts and *Il Gazzettino* and *La Gazzetta dello Sport.*

There was another paper with a heavy black headline about a wife who had killed her husband and run away. Her name caught Mary's eye, *Dottoressa Lucia Costanza.* Wasn't that the woman Homer had written to? Surely not! It couldn't possibly be *their* dottoressa, the distinguished woman who had written back such a courteous letter, expressing her welcome in almost perfect English, with only an occasional charming mistake.

Which way now? Should she cross the bridge into the *sestiere* of San Polo? No, she would leave that for another day. Instead she turned right in a flood of tourists, then left, then right again. Soon she was lost, but she didn't care. After all, she had sworn to follow her nose.

For the rest of the day she wandered without direction, photographing church after church, square after square, rejoicing in side streets where laundry was suspended high overhead, rosy sheets like canopies of heaven, dangling aprons with fluttering strings. When a pulley creaked, she was just in time to catch a hand reaching out to pin a white cloth on the line.

Homesickness was forgotten. Entranced, she drifted north, then west into the *sestiere* of Cannaregio. What was this church? It didn't matter. It was festooned with gesturing sculpture, frenzies of white marble against the sky. *Push the button.* She crossed bridges and found herself in dead ends, then fumbled her way into a broad street full of shoppers. There was a noisy murmur of talk and fragrant whiffs of bread, cigarettes, vanilla, chewing gum. Grapes and pears were arranged in front of a shop like works of art. So were samples of dry pasta in a window— green *tagliatelle agli spinaci,* black *pasta al nero di seppia,* brown *pasta al cacao.*

Heading north again she followed a long *fondamenta* beside the Rio de la Misericordia. By now it was late afternoon, and the tide was rising. Water slopped over the rim of the canal. Mary edged her way along the *fondamenta,* keeping close to the housefronts. When she came to another bridge she crossed it, and found herself in the Ghetto Nuovo, where the pavement was dry.

Yes, of course. This was it, the original ghetto. She had read about the history of the Jews in Venice. It was a long and cruel story. As members of a despised race they had been confined to this little island, an abandoned iron foundry called the Ghetto, and permitted out only at certain hours.

Mary wandered across the square to a wall covered with bronze reliefs, rugged images of cattle cars and crematories. Had Jews been herded into death camps from this city too? Appalled, she murmured it aloud, "Not here too?"

"*Sì, sì,*" said a voice close behind her.

She turned to see a big man in an old-fashioned black hat. He had a full black beard, crisp and curling. "*Anche qui,*" he said. "Here too."

Mary looked back at the cattle cars, and said simply, "How many? *Quanti?*"

The rabbi frowned, and said nothing for a moment. But he was only translating Italian numbers into English. "Two hundred," he said, and his scowl deepened as he mumbled to himself, "*Quaranta sei.*" Then with a triumphant smile he put it all together. "Two hundred and forty!" Turning away he lifted his hat and added, "Six."

Feebly Mary said, "*Grazie.*" She backed up and lifted her camera and took a picture of the cattle cars.

It was the last shot. The film buzzed backward. She put in new film. She was hungry and exhausted. She wandered across another bridge into the Ghetto Vecchio, took a few more pictures, and gave up. Oh, God, it was a long way back!

Beyond the Ghetto Vecchio the water began again. The tide had risen. There was nothing to do but wade. But the main shopping street was dry and full of people coming and going. At San Marcuola Mary boarded a downstream vaporetto and sank into a seat. At once she rummaged in her bag for her notebook and tried to make a list of everything she had seen, all the pictures she had taken.

It was no use. She didn't know where she had been because she had been following her nose, obeying every impulsive whim to go this way rather than that, attracted by the vista from a bridge, or a view of another bridge, or a campanile, or a hand flinging open a shutter. There was no way to make a list. It was all a jumble.

⁂

While the water rose and rose, Dorothea Wellesley had been out shopping. Now she lay on her bed, her galoshes draining on the hot-air register. She was talking on the phone, complaining to an old school friend in Boston. "It's perfectly disgraceful. After a thousand years, wouldn't you think this city would know how to deal with the water of the Adriatic? And the predictions for November are simply appalling."

"But, Dottie, why don't you come home?" Francie's voice was perfectly clear, having whizzed up from Mount Vernon Street to a satellite poised over the Atlantic, then ricocheted down to the Salizada del Pignater. "Now that dear Giorgio is gone, why should you stay in Italy a moment longer?"

"Oh, Francie, you don't understand. I have a sacred trust. Dear Henrietta's poor child, little Ursula. She's a disobedient, fractious and willful little girl, thoroughly spoiled by her father. She needs my loving discipline. And what's more"—Dorothea's voice sank to a melodramatic whisper, faithfully transmitted by the satellite— "who knows, Francie, what might go on in this house, if I were not here to preserve a wholesome family atmosphere?"

She could hear Francie's horrified intake of breath. "Oh, Dottie, you don't mean that your son-in-law—?"

"I do indeed," said Dorothea.

# CHAPTER 16

✂

H omer enjoyed the company of Samuele Bell. He sensed
in Sam a nature severer than his own. Sam was at the
same time amused, self-effacing, and contemptuous.
The contempt wasn't out of malice. It was disappointment in a
world that should have been better, that knew perfectly well
how to be better, but stubbornly refused to improve. The only
way to survive in such a world was to laugh at it, and Sam did.

But it was odd about Sam. In some mysterious way he was
different from the man Homer had met in Massachusetts, more
reckless and impulsive. Well, it took one to know one. Homer
was reckless and impulsive himself.

It was clear that Sam's recklessness was increasing. Lately, just
for the last few days, there had been a crescendo of wild wit in
his talk, as though he were throwing up a dazzling mist over
something pent-up and excruciating. A powerful set of pincers
was wrenching at Sam's gizzard, but what it might be, Homer
didn't have a clue.

They were relaxing in Sam's beautiful sitting room after an
exhausting day of listening to scholarly papers by conference
participants. "I've got two lists," said Sam, leaning back in his
chair, sipping orange juice. "A list of Bores—that's Bores with
a capital B—and a list of bastards."

Homer's orange juice had gin in it. "Bastards! Also with a
capital B? Would you like suggestions for new members?"

They settled down to a discussion of candidates. Some of the
conference participants came immediately to mind. There were
various levels of bores, Sam explained, including Bores Third

Class, Second Class, and First Class, and then a pinnacle class at the top, the Supreme Bore of the World.

"What about bastards?" said Homer. "Are they in categories too?"

"Not yet. *Bastardi* are—what do you call it?—generic. They're all ghastly to the same degree."

"What about Professor Himmelfahrt?" suggested Homer. "Oh, God, Sam, I could have told you to turn his paper down. I know him of old. Talk about bores."

Sam gazed at the ceiling and narrowed his eyes and considered. "I'd rate him Bore First Class, I think, no more."

"We ought to hand out certificates on the last day of the conference," said Homer, pouring himself another drink.

At that moment the door opened and Mrs. Wellesley walked in. She smiled brilliantly at Homer and extended her hand. There was something grandiose in the gesture, as if she expected him to kiss it. He shook it clumsily. "Oh, Professor Kelly, what do you think of my new work? It's just been delivered by the frame shop." She giggled. "I suppose you think it's quite horrible."

"Your new work?" Homer looked at the new picture on the wall. It certainly was horrible. It was an insult to the old maps and the painting by Paolo Veneziano on the opposite wall. Mrs. Wellesley had cut a photograph of a French cathedral into pieces, and then she had pasted the pieces on a square of canvas in an exploding pattern, adding painted streaks of orange fire.

Sam jumped into the breach and rescued Homer. "Oh, yes, Dorothea, it's very good. What cathedral is that? It's not—?"

"Chartres? Of course it is. I cut it all to pieces. Kaboom!"

The Supreme Bore of the World went on and on, pointing to this feature and that, while Homer listened politely and made vague remarks of appreciation—*Yes, I see, mmm, yes, how nice, yes, yes, very nice.*

He was careful not to meet Sam's eye.

✂

There was no longer much of a problem with high water. The moon had drifted away from its direct lineup with the sun, and therefore Venice enjoyed a respite. But everyone knew there was no way of stopping it from waxing to a dangerous state of perfect fullness in two weeks' time, and then of course the tides would rise again.

"Experts warn that *acqua alta* will be far worse next time," said the handsome weather reporter, staring gloomily at the camera in one of the television studios in Palazzo Labia.

The future rise and fall of *acqua alta* in the city of Venice did not matter to the speakers and participants in Sam Bell's great conference. They were all leaving, one by one and in clusters. The last to depart were a couple of art historians from Boston University. Sam conducted them to the water taxi that would carry them to the airport on the mainland.

"Oh, God, I don't want to go," said Art Historian Number One, abandoning the dignity of his status as president of five learned societies.

"It's such a gorgeous—well, you know," said Art Historian Number Two, normally a sober and phlegmatic man. "I mean, it's like a dream."

Sam couldn't blame them. Their last moments in the city were smack in the middle of the most famous postcard view in Venice, the Piazzetta with the Ducal Palace on one side, the Marciana on the other, and the tall columns of Saint Theodore and the lion of Saint Mark rising in the middle, while a flotilla of gondolas bobbed gently in the water below the Molo. Another

flood of excited tourists meandered beside the garden, buying
trinkets at the souvenir stands and taking pictures of each other
against the noble spread of the lagoon.

Art Historian Number One bought a shiny pillow stamped
with a view of San Marco, Art Historian Number Two a small
plastic gondola. Then, regretfully, they stepped into the water
taxi. Sam lifted down their baggage and paid the man at the
wheel, hoping the enormous sum would look acceptable on the
list of conference expenses.

It was over. The splendid Venetian conference in the Biblioteca Marciana dedicated to the manuscripts of Cardinal Bessarion and the printed books of Aldus Manutius was now part
of history. Thank God, the conference proceedings would be
edited by someone else. The books would remain on exhibition
for another six weeks. Sam's work was done.

Slowly and a little painfully, he made his way back to the Marciana. In the entry he had to adjust his dazzled eyes to the dark-
ness. He smiled at Signora Di Stefano, the dragon in her lair,
and trudged up the two flights to his office.

"You look tired," said his secretary, looking at him with concern. "Well, no wonder." Signora Pino was an elderly woman,
chosen long ago to ward off the jealousy of his late wife, whose
ears and eyes had been ever alert for treachery. Now that Sam
was a widower he could have hired the prettiest of pretty young
girls to ornament his office, but he liked Signora Pino, and her
job was secure.

"Yes," said Sam. "I think I'll take the rest of the day off."

"Of course. It's only right. I'll take care of things. Have a
good rest. *Sogni d'oro!* Dreams of gold!"

She watched him go. *Povero ragazzo!* He looked so thin and
stooped. The incessant demands of the conference had worn
him out.

But at home there was a surprise. The first package of relics
from the Treasury of San Marco was waiting for him.

"There was an armed guard," exclaimed his mother-in-law.
"He made me sign for it. He wanted to stay until you came

home. I was insulted! Did he think I was going to make off with his precious package? I told him he had another think coming. I asked him what was in it, and, do you know, he wouldn't tell me? I told him you were my son-in-law and that we had no secrets from each other, no secrets whatsoever, but he wouldn't say a word. I insisted that he leave my house, and he made a *dreadful* scene, but at last I literally *pushed* him out."

Sam smiled wearily. He could imagine the cowardice of the guard in the face of his bullying mother-in-law.

He went to his study and put the box on his desk. It was wrapped in brown paper and tied with string, and the knots in the string had been fastened with sealing wax. And yet the package had a disheveled look, as though someone had tried to undo the wrapping without untying the string. Perhaps his mother-in-law in her wounded pride and everlasting inquisitiveness had tried to unwrap it and failed.

Well, no matter. Sam cut the string, removed the wrapping, and opened the box. The relics from San Marco were in numbered packets, each one enclosed in tissue paper. He set them down carefully on a big piece of drawing paper and gently withdrew one of the relics from its packet. It was a piece of sacred wood. All together there were five fragments supposed to have come from the True Cross and ten pieces of unidentified bone.

Had they ever been looked at critically before? For how many hundreds or even thousands of years had they been objects of veneration? How many tragic appeals had been whispered to them, how many agonized prayers? It struck Sam with sudden force that his irreverent hands, picking up and testing these most sacred of Christian relics, were the hands of an infidel. He had to remind himself that it was high time these pieces of bone and fragments of *sacro legno* were looked at with a clear and objective eye.

The questions he would put to them were obvious. Were the bones human? And how old were the pieces of wood? Only if they had existed for nearly two thousand years could they have any claim to authenticity.

The determination of age would require carbon dating, and that was beyond his power. But at least he could determine whether or not the pieces of the cross were all from the same kind of tree. Were they oak or pine or cedar of Lebanon? His microscope could at least tell him that. And what if they were from trees that never existed in that part of the world at all? They would be exposed at last as frauds.

He gazed at the sacred fragments, smiling to himself. If he proved that they were not from the original cross, in other words that they had not been discovered by Saint Helena and distributed all over the believing world, what would people say? Well, of course they would be outraged by the sacrilege.

Putting his head down on his arms, he told himself sleepily that it didn't matter now. In fact it was liberating, in a way, not to care anymore. Sam closed his eyes and began thinking about the Crucifixion.

It had really happened. There was no doubt about that. It had been a genuine historical incident. The man called Jesus had been convicted and brought to a place of execution and crucified. None of the Gospel writers had seen it, but all of them had described the horrible succession of events as though repeating the account of an eyewitness.

Sam fell asleep imagining the cross itself, a few pieces of timber hammered together and stuck in the ground, leaning to one side until shored up by leftover scraps of lumber, and stained over the years with the blood of many a crucified wretch. Perhaps it was true that there had been not one cross but three, in that place called Golgotha. They had lasted for years, the three crosses, looming objects as familiar to passersby as the gallows at a country crossroad—built to endure and exterminate many a filthy beggar to come.

He was awakened by the loud voice of his mother-in-law, chastising Ursula. A moment later there was a soft knock at the

door. When he opened it, his daughter wrapped herself around his waist.

He picked her up and sat down and settled her on his lap. "Papà," she said, leaning against him. "Papà?"

"What is it, little one?"

"What are those things?"

He explained. She listened, then reached out to touch one of the small pieces of wood, but he caught her hand. "No, no, Ursula, you mustn't touch. I promised that no one would handle them but me."

"*Solo tu?*"

"*Solo io.*"

Ursula snuggled closer. "Please, Papà, may I have some money?"

"How much do you want, little one?"

It was a small sum. He gave her what she asked for, and at once she slipped off his knees, beamed at him, and left the room. A moment later she was on her way to her favorite shop.

When she came home her grandmother was at the door. Dismayed, Ursula shoved her package inside her coat, but it was too late.

"Ursula, what have you got there? Your father gave you

money, didn't he? Your father spoils you rotten. Open that bag! Show me."

Ursula tried to squeeze past her, but Mrs. Wellesley put her hands on the bag and tugged. Ursula hung on. For a moment there was a furious wrestling match, and then the package fell to the floor with a smash.

"Oh, no," cried Ursula, falling to her knees. "You've broken it! I hate you!"

Her grandmother stepped back, a little daunted, and said nothing more. But she hadn't given up. Whatever it was, she would find it. She would ransack the child's room until she did.

# C H A P T E R   1 8

⚓

Mary had abandoned her list. She had completely lost track of what her camera had recorded, its shutter flicking open and shut five hundred times. She was floating in a sea of palaces and canals and little bridges with gondolas approaching and gondolas retreating and endless views of churches—the Salute, the Gesuiti, San Zaccaria, Santa Maria Formosa, San Francesco della Vigna, the Church of the Scalzi, Santa Maria dei Miracoli. Churches, churches, there were so many churches. Every little campo had its own, some with naked Gothic vaults, some with ceilings painted with visions of heaven.

Her picture-recording notebook was forgotten. Surely when the pictures were printed, she would remember what they were.

She had at last run out of film. Mary took her exposed rolls to a *tabacchi* on the corner of Salizada del Pignater and bought another dozen. The day was mizzling with rain. It was a good day to spend indoors. She asked Sam's advice.

"Have you seen the Scuola di San Rocco?" he said. "You haven't? Well, go there. Take my word for it."

"But what is it, a church?"

"You'll see. Make Homer come with you. He hasn't seen anything at all. It's in San Polo. Here, let me see your map."

Reluctantly Homer abandoned his plan for another day in the Marciana. Although the conference was over, he was still rejoicing in the exhibition. His kindly friend Sam had ordered the glass cases to be unlocked whenever *il gentilissimo professore dagli Stati Uniti* wished to examine a codex or an Aldine octavo.

Actually, although Homer didn't know it, this laxity was a highly questionable practice, but Sam Bell was beyond caring.

Today Homer had been planning to examine lovingly the first ten books of Livy and a particularly beautiful codex dedicated to the Venetian pope Paul II.

He had a new card index with tabs, and the little tabs were organized under bigger tabs, and everything was arranged according to his old system of colored cards, pink, blue, green, and yellow, because Homer had a grand object in mind. He was planning to write an article for the *Harvard Library Bulletin*— assuming that the editors would accept one from a rank beginner in Renaissance scholarship—an extended review of the magnificent Venetian exhibition, complete with illustrations.

The project was the darling of Homer's heart. Therefore he only reluctantly agreed to accompany Mary to the Scuola Grande di San Rocco.

"I'll come too," said Sam impulsively. And of course it was okay, *tutto bene,* because he would be obeying his new rule. He could do anything now, anything at all, even something as wild and fanciful as taking a day off to see again the most glorious works of art in the city of Venice.

So they set off together, walking from Castello through the *sestiere* of San Marco, avoiding the crowds in the piazza, then crossing the Rialto Bridge and working their way through a labyrinth of streets in San Polo. Suddenly Sam said, "Here we are," and stopped.

Mary and Homer stopped beside him. At once, responding to instinct, Mary lifted her camera and took a picture.

"My God," said Homer, impressed in spite of himself. It was a stage set for an Italian opera. The two white marble buildings in the Campo San Rocco were set at right angles, enclosing a space only big enough for a posturing tenor and a fat soprano. The two facades were a riot of garlanded columns, bristling acanthus leaves, pedimented windows, and marble reliefs.

"Over here," murmured Sam, leading the way into the building on the left. "The other one is the church. Tintoretto spent twenty-four years of his life decorating the Scuola."

They paid their way in, then followed Sam around the ground floor, looking up at the enormous paintings on the walls. Sam said nothing. But as they climbed a splendid staircase to the floor above he said, between gasps, "It always seems so amazing to me, *tanto sorprendente,* that a man with as keen and subtle a mind as Tintoretto's could be so swept away by the Christian myth." He stopped halfway to catch his breath. "And he wasn't just swept away, he was—what's the word?—*esaltato.*"

"Exalted," agreed Mary solemnly. "He certainly was."

"Well, of course"—doggedly Sam climbed the rest of the way—"it's an extraordinary story."

"What is?" said Homer, gasping up the last few steps.

"Oh, you know, the whole thing, the life of Jesus in the New Testament." Sam walked them across the enormous room, uttering sarcasms in a low voice. "The fairy story of the virgin birth. You know perfectly well that all those contemporary mystery religions had virgin births and godlike figures who were sacrificed and resurrected. Here, look at this one, the *Adoration of the Shepherds.*" They stopped and looked at the picture in the corner, and Sam's mockery continued. "There was no star, there were no kings, there were no shepherds kneeling at a manger. There were no tests for virginity in the first century B.C. Nobody knows anything about the mother of Jesus, and yet in Tintoretto's time this entire city was a temple to the Virgin Mary."

"It's a pretty wonderful painting though," whispered Mary. "How noble she is."

"Of course," said Sam. "That's my whole point. That a man of genius can take any absurdity and turn it into something magnificent. Come on, look at Moses striking water from the rock."

They followed him around the room, staring up in awe at the paintings and listening to Sam's whispered blasphemies.

"Hey," said Homer as they completed the circuit, "there's another room over here."

"More of the same." Sam led the way.

It was a chamber called the Albergo. Tintoretto's *Crucifixion* occupied an entire wall. "Oh," said Mary, and then she fell silent. Homer gripped her hand.

"John Ruskin said a clever thing about this one," said Sam softly. "Usually I can't stand Ruskin, he's so bossy and narrow-minded, but this time—"

"What did he say?" murmured Homer.

Sam knew it by heart. *"I must leave this picture to work its will on the spectator, for it is beyond all analysis and above all praise."*

Then he stopped talking, and they stood silently gazing at the tumble of muscular figures erecting the crosses of the thieves, the armed men on horseback, the weeping mourners, the threatening sky, and the towering figure of Christ with his arms spread wide on the cross.

✄

M rs. Wellesley was the perfect stereotype of a mother-in-law—sharp, critical, inquisitive, and demanding. The fact that she was also a supreme bore was another feather in her cap. Sam put up with her patiently, remembering how devotedly she had nursed her dying daughter. And how could he have refused her unselfish offer to stay on after Henrietta's death and take care of Ursula?

Sam had been grateful. He had welcomed his mother-in-law with a newly furnished bedroom, a generous stipend and a comfortable allowance for expenses, and she had taken hold at once.

Therefore how could he cavil at the nature of her care? Ursula was well fed, well bathed, well clothed, supplied with expensive dolls and toys, and taken to suitable films and entertainments. Last summer there had been an expedition to the sandy beaches of the Lido and another to a theme park on the mainland.

"I hope you don't expect me to take the child to church," Dorothea had said at once. "I regard the Christian religion as dangerous for the impressionable mind of a child, especially the papist version here in Italy."

"Oh, no, of course I don't expect it." But Sam had felt a slight misgiving. It was true that he himself made jokes about saints' bones and relics of the True Cross, and here he was putting the matter to the test! And yet his mother-in-law's severe atheism seemed a cold inheritance for a little child.

So for the last three years father and grandmother had been sharing the task of caring for the youngest member of the family.

Mrs. Wellesley provided supervision over the little girl's every move, Sam supplied the affection the child was hungry for, whispering to her in Italian and bouncing her on his knee—

> Al passo, al passo
> Va il cavallo del gradasso.
> Al trotto, al trotto
> Va il caval del giovanotto.
> Al galoppo, al galoppo
> Va il cavallo dell' Ursula, e . . . PUMFETE!

But why was his mother-in-law so inquisitive? Sam found her habit of poking into every nook and cranny of his private life especially irksome. Her nosiness was the reason for the lock he had attached to his study door two years ago. At least now he could keep his papers and correspondence away from her prying eyes, although sometimes Sam wondered if his letters were opened before he picked them up from the hall table. The envelopes sometimes looked a little odd, as though they had been opened very delicately and pasted shut again.

For Dorothea Wellesley the lock was infuriating. It was an insult. How could there be secrets between her and her son-in-law? Did Sam have a secret woman? Someone he didn't dare bring home? Oh, she wouldn't put it past him!

The truth was, Sam's mother-in-law was as suspicious as her daughter had been of his possible erotic adventures. In fact it was Dorothea's warnings about the perfidy of men that had been responsible for Henrietta's wariness. She had been cautioned about voluptuous secretaries, curvaceous librarians, and sultry professional colleagues. She had been frightened into a state of perpetual jealousy. She had confronted Sam with her suspicions at every turn.

Poor dear Henrietta! She was gone now, carried off by a malignancy that had spread from her breasts to her lymph nodes to her liver. But her mother was still on guard. Three years after the death of Sam's wife, Mrs. Wellesley suspected darkly that he was ready for new amorous adventures. He was still so good-looking! And a widower! And a man with an important position! And therefore highly vulnerable to the seductive attentions of women on the make. He might betray Henrietta's memory at any time by sneaking off with some alluring female. Dorothea knew the pitiful prevarications of men. If there was one thing on this earth that she understood from top to bottom, and inside and out, and back to front in all its lust and deceit, it was the opposite sex.

Why did Sam always lock his study door? What secrets lay inside that room? What evidences of infidelity?

The arrival of the mysterious package at last goaded her into action. Dorothea began a campaign of discovery. On the very first day she won a victory. Foolish Sam! On his way upstairs to take a nap he forgot to bring his keys. There they lay, fully exposed on the table in the hall.

Which was the key to his study? Dorothea recognized the house keys and the key to the car that was parked at Piazzale Roma. The Marciana key bore a tag. There was only one left. It must be the one she was looking for.

She snatched it up and ran out of the house. There was a *negozio di ferramenta* around the corner, right next to the Church of San Giovanni in Bragora. Dorothea nipped out of the house and waited at the counter for the proprietor to finish counting out screws for one customer and helping another to choose an aluminum ladder. At last she presented her key and asked for two copies.

The errand took too long. When she got back, Sam was just emerging from his nap, looking more exhausted than ever.

"Oh, Sam, dear, I hope you're feeling better?" Dorothea backed up to the hall table and artfully dropped the borrowed key.

His face looked wasted from lack of sleep. "I'll just make myself a cup of coffee."

Dorothea watched him trudge away in the direction of the kitchen. Quickly then, she reattached the borrowed key to the key ring. Then she hurried into her bedroom and laid the new keys on her dresser next to the photograph of Henrietta as a bride.

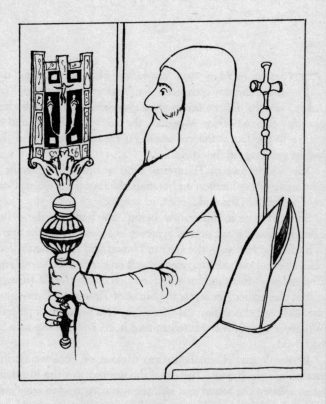

*In the Gallerie dell'Accademia a Byzantine reliquary with
fragments of the True Cross is displayed beside a portrait of
Cardinal Bessarion.*

# CHAPTER 20

✂

*T*he more Mary went exploring with her camera, the more she was convinced that Venice was the city of Tintoretto. His paintings were everywhere, in church after church—in San Giorgio Maggiore, the Salute, the Frari—and of course in the Ducal Palace, where his *Paradise* was one of the largest paintings in the world.

She was in awe of Tintoretto. One morning, looking for a new route of exploration on her map, she found the words *Casa del Tintoretto* in the middle of Cannaregio.

She had been in this *sestiere* before. She had seen the desiccated body of Santa Lucia of Syracuse in a glass coffin like Snow White's, she had seen the Ghetto Nuovo and the Ghetto Vecchio, and stopped at a newsstand for a Paris edition of the *Herald Tribune*.

But she hadn't run across the house of Tintoretto. Everything she had read about him was admirable. Did he live in a palace? Whatever it was, she wanted to find it, to imagine the way he had lived.

It wasn't easy. Cannaregio was a maze of little wandering streets and dead ends. The canal she wanted was the Rio della Sensa. When she found it at last, she was surprised to see a gulf where the water should have been. This part of the rio had been drained. In place of the sparkling jade-green water running so pleasantly in all the other canals, there was only a muddy crevasse.

Crossing the bridge over the empty gully, she looked for the Campo dei Mori. It had to be here somewhere. Yes, of course,

NE PRAETEREAS VIATOR
JAC. ROBUSTI QVI TINTORETTO
DOMVM VETVSTAM
INDE TABVLAE INNVMERAE
MENTE PENICILLO IPSVS PERACRI
AE FABRE ELABORATAE
PVBLICE PRIVATIMQ. ASPECTABILES
LATE PRODIERVNT
HOC TE RESCIRE JVVABIT
CVRA PRESENTIS DOMINI
MDCCCXLII

3398

here it was, the Square of the Moors. One of them was set into the corner, a clumsy carved figure wearing a kind of turban. Well, fine, but where was Tintoretto's house?

Mary looked vaguely left and right, then paused to watch two families with dogs confront each other in the square. The little terrier stood rigid and barked. *"Ma dai, ma dai!"* chastised its owner. The other dog was old and shaggily dignified. The two groups moved off together, their dogs trotting beside them, tails floating high.

*Come now, concentrate.* Mary opened her map, which was coming apart at the folds, put her finger on the Casa del Tintoretto, folded the map again, and set off firmly to the right.

❈

Doctor Richard Henchard had been inspecting his treasure. He had opened up the entire wall with the wrecking bar and moved everything out of the hiding place into the closet, and then he had hung a curtain over the ruined wall. For the moment he left the newspaper-wrapped packages alone and concentrated on the golden objects, the scrolls and the plates and cups and candlesticks and the funny-looking things like little castles, and of course the painting, most especially the painting. It was very old and very fine. Could it possibly be a Titian? If so, it was worth millions of lire, billions, *trillions.*

Like Sam Bell on the other side of the city, Richard Henchard had attached a lock to the door to keep out prying eyes. It was only a padlock, but it would do the trick. Then he hired an expensive locksmith to change the lock on the street door in case that noodle-brained female, Signorina Pastora in the Agenzia, should take it into her head to rent the place again.

The question was, how to turn all this splendor into cash? Well, there was no hurry. He would explore various avenues. The gold objects should probably be melted down. Should the painting go to an art dealer in Paris? And how could he preserve anonymity? The things were absolutely, undeniably his own, but it might be necessary to produce documentary proof of legal possession. And that might be tricky, very tricky indeed.

Henchard clasped the padlock shut, pocketed the key, descended to the street, and locked the outer door. Turning away he at once caught sight of a woman with a camera. He watched as she took a picture, then another. Why didn't she stop? She was moving along the *fondamenta,* photographing every house.

Who was she? Ordinary tourists wouldn't take so many pictures. If she was just a tourist who was interested in the painter's house, why was she photographing the entire row?

Christ, now she had reached his own place—she was shooting the very window behind which his treasure was hidden. Fortunately the window was heavily curtained. Whoever had created the hiding place had nailed a blanket over the glass, a double thickness of wool. The blanket was furry with dust, like the contents of the chamber, and speckled with black strands from the crumbling ceiling, but it still kept out the light. No sunshine had entered the little room for years, and nothing could be seen from outside.

But she was still staring up at the window through the lens of her camera. Goddamn the woman! What the hell was she doing?

At last she lowered the camera. She was turning to him, looking at him. *"Permesso, signore, posso andare internamente, nella casa del Tintoretto?"*

Her accent was American, not English. He moved toward her, smiling, and spoke in his native tongue. "Can one go into Tintoretto's house? I'm sorry, but it's not a museum. It's a private house."

Mary touched a button on her camera to close the shutter. Abandoning her labored Italian, she said, "I see. That's too bad."

She was a tourist then? Only a tourist? "You're visiting from America?"

"Yes." Mary smiled. "My husband and I are here for six weeks. We're teachers on sabbatical."

"Sabbatical? I see. You're on vacation." Perhaps she was not simply a tourist after all. "Oh, signora," he said, remembering a fragment of history, "perhaps you'd like to see the painter's church?"

"Tintoretto's church?" She looked pleased. Her cheeks were plump and pink. "Does it have some of his paintings?"

Henchard didn't have the faintest idea. "Oh, yes, many paintings. The Church of the Madonna dell' Orto. It's not far away. May I show it to you?"

He watched as the American woman thought it over. It was apparent that she was a virtuous woman, highly respectable and intelligent. Mentally removing her blouse and unhooking her brassiere, he could see that she was deep-breasted, a veritable goddess.

"Permit me to introduce myself," he said easily, offering up a pseudonym. "My name is Richard Visconti. I am a doctor, but this is my day off." Well, of course that was a lie. It meant he'd have to cancel an appointment, but that would be a relief anyway because the patient was a sad case, a man with a terminal carcinoma.

She had made up her mind. She was smiling broadly. "Why, yes, that's very kind of you."

He bowed, and lifted his arm in a courtly gesture. *"Andiamo!"*

The space between the houses and the edge of the *fondamenta* above the muddy excavation was narrow. Henchard took Mary's arm with an air of courteous male guardianship, guiding her past a place where the paving stones had been taken up and piled at one side.

"My name is Mary Kelly," she said, glancing at him with that air of easy frankness so typical of American women.

*"Buongiorno,* Mrs. Kelly. Or is it Doctor Kelly? Instinct tells me you have a doctor's degree." She grinned and didn't deny it, and he made up his mind to ask her to lunch after the tour of the church.

Richard Henchard was an old hand at playing a fish. This one required the most delicate lure, the gentlest of tugs on the line.

Catalogue Room, Museo Correr

⌘

Homer was in the kitchen of the apartment on the top floor of Sam Bell's house when Mary walked in. She was a little tipsy after drinking three glasses of wine in the company of Doctor Visconti.

He was eager to tell her about his afternoon in the catalog room of the Biblioteca Correr. "Mary, it was amazing. They don't have any computerized records at all, just a couple of kind librarians. Everything was on cards, good old catalog cards, and when they couldn't find the one for the book I wanted, they pulled out a shoebox from under the counter."

"A shoebox? Oh, surely not a shoebox?"

"What did you see today, my darling?"

"Well, let's see. I saw Tintoretto's house in Cannaregio, only I couldn't go in. I just saw it on the outside. And the Church of the Madonna dell'Orto. It was Tintoretto's parish church, that's why I wanted to see it."

"I see. It was another Tintoretto day, is that it? Those paintings of his really got to you."

"Oh, right, they certainly did. Oh, Homer, excuse me. I'm worn out. I've got to lie down."

Dropping onto the bed, Mary wondered why she had said nothing to Homer about having lunch with Richard Visconti. She didn't know why. She just hadn't wanted to, that was all there was to it.

✖

*T*he month of November began with rain. Sam held his umbrella low over his head and kept to the inland side of the Riva degli Schiavoni, away from the brimming *bordo* of the lagoon.

He had a lot on his mind. At least, thank God, the conference was over. But although his new sense of carelessness had been liberating for a while, it had stopped working. He cared too much about too many things.

There was item number one, but there was no point in thinking about that.

Item number two was the disappearance of Lucia Costanza, but there was no point in thinking about that either.

Item number three was more possible, his mission to reverse the Venetian belief in fraudulent relics, in the beseeching power of lighted candles, in the sanctimonious prayers broadcast over Radio Maria, *una voce cristiana nella tua casa*. With the help of Lucia Costanza and with the astonishing permission of Father Urbano and the cardinal patriarch, Sam was now putting the relics to the test.

So far in his investigations he had determined that the so-called pieces of the True Cross had come from several different kinds of wood. It was a gratifying discovery. But how old were they? That was important too. Sam didn't have the equipment to carbon-date the fragments, so he would have to have the permission of the cardinal patriarch to take them out of his house under guard and carry them across town to the university.

Item number four was the Marciana. Sam was ashamed of the

way he'd been neglecting his duties. During the months of preparation for the conference and the exhibition, and then during the intense week of the conference itself, his ordinary work had fallen far behind. His boss, the director of the Marciana, had made a few gentle remarks, almost too courteous to be understood as complaints.

And Signora Pino kept looking at Sam in melancholy urgency with an important letter in her hand or a paper to sign or a contract for vastly expensive repairs that urgently needed his signature. This morning she reminded him of his meeting with the Piazza Council. "Oh, of course," said Sam. "Thank you. I had forgotten."

The Piazza Council was the new group of functionaries from all the major institutions in the neighborhood—the Biblioteca Marciana, the Palazzo Ducale and the Museo Correr, the office of the Soprintendenza ai Beni Artistici e Storici di Venezia, the Procuratie di San Marco, and of course the Basilica di San Marco itself.

They had begun to meet regularly in the Ducal Palace in the Hall of the Council of Ten, a fabulous chamber with a melancholy history and a painted ceiling writhing with gold moldings. This morning the regular members of the Piazza Council were joined by the mayor of Venice, representing the Venice City Council, and by employees of AMAV—the Venetian Environmental Multiservices Corporation—as well as by others from the Consorzio Venezia Nuova, a consortium of private contractors.

The deliberations of the Piazza Council were perhaps doomed from the start, because there was bad feeling between the city council and the rich and powerful Consorzio Venezia Nuova.

But the problem of high water in the piazza was a severe one, and it called for heroic efforts by somebody, somehow, and as soon as possible.

The mayor laid it out in plain words. "As you all know, the piazza is at the lowest point in Venice. It is also the busiest part of the city. The dangerous month of November is nearly here, and the lagoon is already spilling over the Molo twice a day, in spite of the fact that this is the time of neap tide. Let us not forget that the *moon*"—the mayor lowered his voice to a deep throb and looked grimly around the table—"the *moon* will be full again in only seven days."

They looked at each other solemnly, feeling the weight of the earth's dangerous satellite hovering over their heads. The mayor held up a calendar and tapped it with his finger. "This is the date of the highest autumn spring tide. The meteorologists are warning that the stormy forecast and the probability of high winds in the near future may create the worst problem in years."

"And we all know what that means," sighed Father Urbano. "Sixty centimeters of water in the piazza."

"The fact is," said the man from AMAV, looking dolefully at Father Urbano, "we're afraid of a return of the inundation of 1966."

At this gloomy prediction the director of the Correr started out of his chair. "Nineteen sixty-six! You can't mean it, not again! But the water was one hundred twenty-five centimeters deep in the piazza in 1966!"

The mayor seemed to take pleasure in apocalyptic pronouncements. His voice became even more sepulchral as he drew forth another chart showing the distribution of high water throughout the city. "This map has been provided by our friends in AMAV," he said, smiling at their representative. "These areas in yellow remain relatively dry, whereas these in light blue"—he tapped the chart—"are inundated, and this one in dark blue—" He pointed at the piazza and fell silent. There was no need to finish the sentence.

"If *only*," said the man from the Consorzio Venezia Nuova, "we had been permitted to install our floodgates at the three points of entry of the Adriatic into the lagoon, this problem would never again arise. As you are all well aware, our scale model has been working perfectly. We are ready to go."

It was a sore point. The mayor started to say something, then controlled himself.

Sam Bell looked up at the ceiling painting of two beautiful fat women by Veronese, *Venice Receiving the Ducal Cap from Juno*, and wished the gods and goddesses hovering over the city were interested in more important matters.

He spoke up. "Aren't we the lucky ones! It's our privilege to be flooded the deepest." He looked around the table. "But we've all been through it before. I think we've all learned how to protect our buildings from *acqua alta*. In the Marciana, *per esempio,* we have a system of four teams. They are trained to go to work at once in cases of flood emergency. But of course I'll talk to the director and see what else we can do. Thank you for the warning."

"As an acting procurator of San Marco," said a stranger in a loud voice, "I will also take whatever steps may be necessary."

Sam glanced down the table and realized that the man was not a total stranger. Lucia Costanza had introduced him as her assistant, Signor Bernardi. Then, later, on the day after her disappearance, *quest' idiota* had intimated that she was a thief. Was this upstart pretending to take her place? Sam sank back in his chair as Bernardi talked interminably, managing to be imprecise and vague while enumerating all the measures that they in the Palazzo Patriarcale were going to take against high water, namely measures 1, 2, 3, 4, 5, and 6.

Sam stopped listening. It occurred to him that Bernardi deserved a place in his Society of Bores. The more the man droned on, the higher Sam raised him in the hierarchy, inventing dazzling upper reaches. When Bernardi sat down he had achieved the level of Knight Errant Bore in the Thirty-third Degree.

## CHAPTER 22

※

Ursula had a doll. It was an anorexic platinum blond Barbie doll. To the child it was another self, a friend, something to cherish.

Her grandmother loathed the doll, and refused to give Ursula pieces of fabric for the making of doll dresses. "Really, Ursula, that creature is a piece of outrageous commercial exploitation. I can't bear to look at it."

One day Mary Kelly found Ursula making the doll a dress. "Oh, Ursula, what a pretty doll. What's her name?"

Ursula looked at her warily. "It's Ursula."

"Ursula? The same as yours? Well, I like the two Ursulas." Mary sat down and watched the child pull down over the doll's head a bunchy outfit of gauzy blue cloth. The side seams had not been stitched. The dress was held together with big X's sewn into the corners.

Mary reached out and touched it. "What lovely material. If you have more of it, I could help you make something else."

Ursula's face broke into a wide smile. Without a word she jumped up and ran to her room. When she came back she was dragging one of her own dresses, a flouncy pale blue article with ruffles. It looked expensive. A large piece had been hacked out of the skirt.

Mary guessed that the little girl would soon be in terrible trouble. "I'll tell you what, why don't you and I go shopping and buy a few pieces of pretty stuff? You know, a little velveteen, and some ribbon and lace edging?"

"Oh, yes," breathed Ursula.

"But first—may I?" Mary took the doll. "Look, if you made some darts, the dress would fit better." With Ursula's permission she took the dress off the doll and explained. The little girl grasped the idea at once, and bounced up to find a paper of pins.

They were hard at work, teacher and pupil, when Mrs. Wellesley burst in, her painting materials under her arm, and complained bitterly about the weather. "I had to stop in the middle," she said, showing Mary a sheet of blotched watercolor paper. "I couldn't finish." Then suddenly her attention sharpened, and she stared at the vandalized dress.

At once there was an uncomfortable scene. It appeared that the dress had been a birthday present from Mrs. Wellesley. And then she began on the doll. "Oh, that horrible creature! Ursula, where's that really beautiful doll I bought you on Via Madonetta Meloni? Oh, Mrs. Kelly, it's the loveliest doll. Go get it, dear. I want to show it to Mrs. Kelly."

Ursula got up slowly and retreated to her room. She did not come back. It was soon evident that another crisis was impending, and Mary excused herself. As she headed for the stairs she heard the brazen voice of Mrs. Wellesley shrieking at her granddaughter, "Ursula? Where are you? What on *earth* are you doing?"

# CHAPTER 23

✄

Mary no longer wandered alone around the city of Venice. These days her explorations were often accompanied by the good-looking doctor she had met in front of the house of Tintoretto. They met again the day after, to climb the spiral staircase of the Palazzo Contarini del Bovolo. At the top of the winding stairs there was a broad view of the city. Bulky in the foreground rose the framework for the new walls of the concert hall of La Fenice, which had been destroyed by fire.

Henchard stood beside her, identifying landmarks, pointing out church towers.

"Doctor Visconti," said Mary, looking dreamily at the bulbous domes of San Marco, "are you sure you have time for this? I should think your schedule would be too full of—what?—surgery and appointments with patients, and—"

"No, no, I have plenty of time. Surgery's first thing in the morning. Ordinary appointments are in the afternoon, but there aren't very many right now. At the moment my fellow citizens seem to be fairly healthy. Except, of course, for a few sad cases. There are always some of those." Henchard was standing close to Mary, his shoulder against hers. He turned and said gently, "Please call me Richard."

Again he took her to lunch, this time at a famous place, the Osteria ai Assassini.

"What a horrible name," said Mary. "Where does it come from?"

"I don't have the faintest idea." Henchard lifted his glass. "To the assassins!"

She touched her glass against his. "To their victims!"

They made other journeys around the city, exploring the Naval Museum and the Arsenal and a couple of palaces where famous people had died, Ca' Rezzonico (Browning) and Vendramin-Calergi (Verdi). Next week, promised Henchard, they would go by vaporetto to the island of Murano to see the blowing of glass.

It was all perfectly innocent. It hardly seemed worthwhile to say anything to Homer about it, and Mary didn't.

For the days when Richard was too busy to join her, Mary set herself a new project, making friends with Sam Bell's daughter, Ursula. The poor child seemed so bereft. Her closed little face was sadder than ever. "Tell you what," said Mary, "let's go find those pretty pieces of fabric. I discovered a shop near Piazza San Marco. Would you like that?"

The little girl's face brightened. "Can we feed the pigeons?"

Mary hated the pigeons in Piazza San Marco. "Why, of course. We'll buy them some popcorn."

The vast square teemed with people. It was a lovely day. Tour guides conducted their flocks around the square. There were travelers from Munich—*Siehe den löwen mit flügel? Es ist der löwe des Heiligen Mark*—and a group of senior citizens from Paris—*La Basilique Saint Marc est la plus célèbre eglise d'Europe. Admirez les quatre chevaux!*—and schoolchildren from Verona—*Questa chiesa è la Basilica di San Marco, costruita nel nono secolo per ospitare il corpo del santo.* OK, *ragazzi, avanti!*

Mary poured popcorn into Ursula's hands and she held them out for the pigeons.

They came at once, with a loud flapping of wings, landing on her hands, her arms and shoulders, pecking each other, snatching her popcorn. The little girl was ecstatic. Her laughing face was rosy and chubby.

Mary tried to restrain her dislike for the pigeons, but they were so ugly, so greedy, so spoiled, so fat with the offerings of thousands of tourists. "Ready, Ursula? Shall we go into the church?"

But Ursula hung back, remembering the priest who had said she was too young to kneel and whisper through the curtain. "No, *grazie*."

They moved away, followed by clouds of pigeons, and escaped into the crowded shopping lane called the Mercerie, looking for a place to buy gelato.

"You've got a pretty feather in your hair," said Mary, plucking it off. Ursula took the feather, smiling, and put it back on the top of her head.

*A blessing from above,* thought Mary sentimentally, remembering the sign that had fallen from the sky like a sign of divine favor on the future emperor, the child Claudius. Why wasn't a pigeon feather a lucky omen? Ursula needed all the help she could get.

⋈

Next day after school Ursula stopped again at her favorite shop, because Mrs. Kelly had given her money to pay for pretty ribbons and flower-patterned calico and pink velveteen, and then she wouldn't take back the leftover coins.

"Which is it to be today, little one?" said the man behind the counter.

Ursula considered. She had so many of them now. Only the less attractive ones were left. "Well, that one's okay, I guess," she said at last. *"Grazie."*

✠

# CHAPTER 24

Sam had learned another damning fact about the fragments of wood from the Treasury of San Marco. After consulting a couple of sources in the library of the university—a silly book in English, *The Trees Jesus Loved*, and an exhaustive German treatise, *Den Bäumen des Biblischen Landes*—he had come to the only possible conclusion. None of the little pieces came from trees that grew within a thousand miles of Jerusalem in the first century of the Christian era.

There was no necessity for carbon dating. And there was no need to say anything yet to Father Urbano about the results of his examination, not until all the other relics had been looked at. Among them there might be one or two that were at least plausible.

So these could go back to the Treasury, and he could ask for more. Sam called the number he had been given by Father Urbano. The phone buzzed and paused and buzzed. Somewhere in the depths of San Marco it was ringing and ringing. Sam had a vision of the telephone shrilling right there under the Ascension dome, setting up a clamor throughout all the glittering volumes of golden air. *Answer that!* one of the mosaic angels would shout, opening its tessellated mouth, and another would cry, *It's your turn,* and then Saint Mark would have to rear up out of his sarcophagus and say, *Pronto?*

"*Pronto?*" said the telephone, but it was only Father Urbano.

Sam explained that he was finished with the first relics and would like to exchange them for more.

"Tell me," said Father Urbano eagerly, "what did you find

out?" His voice trembled a little, and Sam guessed how much it mattered.

"I'll tell you when I come. You'll send a guard to come with me?"

"*Certamente.* At once."

But when the carabiniere arrived, Sam wasn't ready. He had to rush back from the Marciana, apologize to the waiting officer, lead him upstairs into his study and gather up the relics in a hurry. Then they marched together along the Riva to the Piazzetta and the basilica, the carabiniere carrying the relics in a cardboard box sealed with mailing tape, holding it delicately in front of his stomach with both hands.

The north entry into the basilica was sloppy with water, but the sacristy was up several steps and perfectly dry. Here Sam and the young officer watched Father Urbano open the tissue-paper packets of *Sacro Legno* and count, "*Uno, due, tre, quattro.*" He looked up at Sam. "Only four?"

"But there should be five," said the officer. "I brought you five last month, remember?"

"You must have left one at home," said Father Urbano, smiling doubtfully at Sam.

Sam was dumbfounded. "I don't think so." They were looking at him with questioning faces. "But, good Lord, I must have."

"And there are only nine pieces of bone," said Father Urbano, opening another packet and counting. "Didn't I give you ten?"

"Of course you did." Sam gazed at the pitiful little bones. "I don't know what to say. They must be still at home."

"*Bene,*" said the officer. "We'll go and see." His voice was pleasant, but Sam knew there'd be hell to pay if the lost relics were not returned.

The journey was fruitless. Sam ransacked his study, but no other bone was to be found, nor any other fragment of sacred wood.

"I will make a report to Father Urbano," said the officer, his face expressionless.

But then, to Sam's astonishment, the priest was magnanimous. He called to say, "My dear Sam, I trust you. And to prove it, I have a surprise. The curator of the treasures in the Scuola di San Giovanni Evangelista has agreed to send me their reliquary. You know, the famous one containing their own piece of the True Cross."

"You mean the one in the cycle of paintings in the Accademia, *that* reliquary? The one that performed all those miracles?"

"That's the one."

Sam was flabbergasted. "Oh, thank you, Father. Of course I'll be more careful than ever. Did you tell them I've lost some of your relics?"

"No, no, that's just between us for the moment. The officer has been sworn to secrecy. Once again, Sam, the loan is only for a month."

"But aren't you putting yourself in danger of—forgive me, Father—burning at the stake, or at least excommunication? I mean, if anything should happen to their glorious reliquary?"

Father Urbano's voice turned solemn. "I'm not doing this for you, my dear Sam. Nor even for the sake of the truth. I can't help thinking of my friend Dottoressa Costanza, who made the original request. I honor it for her sake."

*In the Scuola di San Giovanni Evangelista a famous reliquary contains a fragment of the True Cross. Its miracles are celebrated in a cycle of paintings in the Gallerie dell'Accademia.*

# CHAPTER 25

✄

Next day Sam took the afternoon off to visit the Accademia. He wanted to refresh his memory about the painted miracles of the relic of the True Cross, the one he was about to examine.

He took Mary Kelly along. She met him in his office, and together they boarded the vaporetto near the foot of the Piazzetta. That is, they boarded it after Sam missed his footing and nearly fell off the floating dock.

Mary grabbed him, and so did a couple of passengers, and so did the girl with the rope in her hand. "Are you all right, Sam?" said Mary, looking at him with concern.

He was embarrassed. "Of course I'm all right." Balancing himself with his legs spread wide apart, he gripped the railing as the vaporetto shuddered away from the dock.

It was only a few stops to the small square in front of the Accademia. When they disembarked, Sam bought a *Gazzettino* at the kiosk and glanced at it quickly for any scrap of information about Dottoressa Costanza.

"Any news?" said Mary, who had lost track of what was going on in the world.

"Nothing important," said Sam, folding the paper and stuffing it in his pocket.

The little square was busy with tourists. They were buying postcards and souvenirs and taking pictures of the gondoliers who stood there idly, smoking and waiting for customers.

"*Quanto costa?*" said a boy, egged on by his girlfriend. They were part of a crowd of kids on holiday from Naples.

The two gondoliers were punctiliously dressed in navy blue uniforms with sailor collars. Red ribbons dangled from their straw hats. One wore glasses, the other had a gold earring. At once they began bantering with the boy and his girlfriend. Everybody laughed. The boy shook his head. The price was too high.

Sam and Mary watched as the gondoliers flirted with the girls and adjusted their prices. There was a whispered conference, and at last the girls were handed down into one of the gondolas, taking their places in the thronelike chairs or stepping tippily across the first gondola into the second. The boys stepped down after them. Everyone was pleased. They were laughing. The gondoliers tossed away their cigarettes and took up their poles.

Mary smiled too, and turned to Sam, but he had moved away across the square. He was talking to another pair of kids, also in costume. The boy wore a grubby brocaded coat and a pair of silken knee-pants, unfastened at the knees and drooping down his shins. The laces of his sneakers trailed on the pavement. The girl had a pink skirt puffed out at the sides like panniers. It was too long. She was stepping on the muddy hem.

They were selling concert tickets, speaking in a mixture of English and Italian. *"Un concerto nella chiesa dei Frari! Monteverdi, Handel, Bach! Choruses, soloists, orchestre!"*

"We'll all go, shall we?" said Sam, and he shelled out thousands of lire. Mary quickly paid the Kellys' share, then scrabbled in her bag for more thousands to pay her way into the Accademia.

Sam hurried her up the stairs. "You can see all this later," he said, rushing her down a corridor.

"Oh, all right," said Mary, glancing left and right, catching tantalizing glimpses of famous works of art.

He slowed down at last. "Here we are."

The room was devoted to eight huge paintings of the miracles performed by a relic of the True Cross belonging to the Scuola di San Giovanni Evangelista. It was the very same relic that was about to be entrusted to Sam Bell.

Mary was entranced. "Sam, what's this one all about? Why are they all swimming in the water?"

"It was a religious procession," explained Sam. "The brothers were carrying the cross over the bridge when it fell in the water. Of course they all jumped in to save it, and one of them managed to grab it." He glanced at Mary. "They seemed to think it was a miracle."

"Mmm," said Mary. "I see." They moved on, and at once she was excited. "Oh, Sam, how wonderful! It's the Square of Saint Mark. It looks just the same right now."

"Well, perhaps not quite," murmured Sam. He pointed. "Do you see the reliquary, there under the canopy?"

"Oh, yes, all gold, how beautiful. Where's the miracle?"

"The kneeling man, there on the right. He's praying for the healing of his injured son back home. Afterward, guess what? His son was okay. How's that for a miracle?"

Mary laughed. "Well, *they* must have thought it was a miracle. I mean, just look at all the trouble and expense they went to. I'm glad they did. It's a magnificent painting. Okay, what's next?"

"This one's a sort of anti-miracle." Sam looked up at the painting, which was crowded with active figures and gondolas and people looking out of windows and tall men in red and black robes standing solemnly in the foreground. "It's a funeral procession. They were carrying the reliquary into a church for the funeral of one of the brothers, when it suddenly became so heavy they could hardly carry it."

"Why? What sort of miracle was that?"

"I think it was a case of disrespect. The dead man had not been sufficiently devoted to the relic, so it refused to take part in his funeral." Sam shook his head in cynical wonder. "Queer sort of miracle, if you ask me." He hurried Mary to the other end of the room. "This one's my favorite."

"Well, no wonder." Mary gazed with delight at the wooden

bridge, the crowds of people, the palaces crowned with chimney pots, the gondolas with their elegant gondoliers. "And, oh, Sam, look at the laundry up there against the sky on long poles! What delicious detail! But where's the miracle?"

"It doesn't seem very important, does it? It's up there on the loggia. The man in black is possessed. He's being cured by the relic of the cross." Sam turned to Mary. "Look, *cara mia,* I've got to get back. You stay as long as you like."

"Oh, thank you, Sam. I'm greedy to see all the rest."

Sam found his way back to the grand staircase and walked out of the Accademia. His cynicism about the relic was stronger than ever. The brothers of the confraternity had claimed that their relic alone, unlike other pieces of the True Cross, was *miracolosa,* but on the evidence of these paintings all its wondrous prodigies were a poor lot. Of course it was good that they had inspired these glorious works of art, but as miracles, they were pitiful.

And one of them distressed him, the miracle condemning one member of the brotherhood, the man whose lack of reverence had angered the relic. Sam felt a twinge of personal connection. He too was about to be irreverent. In presuming to touch the golden reliquary with doubting hands would he be showing his own contempt? Would the cross fight back?

Vaporetto number 1 scraped against the floating dock. *"Attenzione,"* cried the girl as she unwound the rope. *"Un momento."*

Sam waited for the flood of disembarking passengers, then stepped on board, thinking how strange it was that his perfectly logical mind could harbor such a thought.

As the vaporetto pulled away he stood at the railing, gazing at the Palazzo Barbaro drifting slowly past, imagining Henry James leaning on one of the balconies, looking back at him. Or perhaps Mrs. Jack Gardner had just this moment turned away from one of the lofty Gothic windows to talk to John Singer Sargent. "Oh, please, Mr. Sargent, do tell me which Venetian palace I should dismantle and carry back to Boston?" Whether they had been morally right or wrong, you had to

admit that they had left a rich purple stain on the air. How alive
they had all been!

Sam moved into the seating compartment of the vaporetto
and found a place to sit down. They were dead now, of course.
All dead.

✂

# CHAPTER 26

The reliquary arrived under guard in a wooden crate. Sam signed for it, lugged it into his study, and locked the door.

It was very large and very gold. The front was adorned with a golden Christ on a golden cross, the back with a golden image of John the Evangelist, patron saint of the Scuola di San Giovanni Evangelista. The reliquary itself was shaped like a cross with crystal arms. The uppermost arm enclosed the *frammento del Lignum Crucis*, the small scrap of wood that was supposed to have come from the cross on which Christ was crucified. Little figures of the mourning Mary and Saint John were flung out at the sides on their own pedestals. Attached to the edges of the reliquary sixteen jewels stuck out into empty air, as though the goldsmith had thought to himself, "Why not pretty it up a little more?"

Sam set it carefully on his desk, then stood back. In the shadowy room it glimmered and glowed. When a ray of morning sunlight struck past the neighboring rooftops of the houses on Salizada del Pignater and slanted through the window, the reliquary flared up like a thousand candles.

Well, that was the goldsmith's art. But as an object of study the tiny piece of *Lignum Crucis* was going to require very sophisticated equipment because it was encased in crystal. Sam had promised Father Urbano that he would not take the reliquary apart. Therefore he had arranged to borrow a more powerful gadget from a biochemist at the university, a microscope that could examine its object with a high degree of resolving power, even through the crystal.

It was two days before Sam had time to go far across the city to the Department of Physics and Chemistry. It was not in the famous palace housing the rest of the university, the Ca' Foscari on the Grand Canal. Instead he had to take Vaporetto #52 all the way around Dorsoduro past the Zattere to the stop at Santa Marta, and then walk a long way to the neighborhood of the Church of San Niccolò. Fortunately both ends of the journey were in parts of the city a few inches higher than the lowest places. Salizada del Pignater was just south of a deeper area around Campo Sant' Antonin, and the Quartiere Santa Marta was entirely in the clear. Sam walked to his destination dry-shod.

"State of the art," said the biochemist proudly, showing off his microscope, instructing Sam in the subtleties of its use. "It's a reflecting microscope, you see, Sam. You'll have a working distance of a good inch, not just a millimeter." Packing it into its case he said, "*Questa maledetta cosa è molto pesante.* It weighs a ton. Too bad you can't bring your object here."

Sam looked doubtfully at the big case and explained, "I wish I could, but I've promised to keep it locked up in my house until it goes back under guard."

"Well, for Christ's sake be careful. I mean, Jesus, Sam, this thing's worth a king's ransom."

"Oh, I will, I promise I will." Sam picked up the case, then set it down again.

"Can you manage it?" said the biochemist, opening the door.

"*Naturalmente.*" Sam picked up the case again with a show of ease. "*Ciao, Carlo. Grazie tante.*"

"*Prego.*"

But the microscope in its thick protective case was almost more than he could manage. Sam grasped the handle with both hands and shuffled out of the building, leaning backward. What kind of superman was Carlo anyway? Had he ever tried to carry it himself?

In the Campo San Niccolò he hailed a student and paid him

to lug the microscope to the vaporetto stop at San Basilio. There he was able to take a water taxi to the Riva and up a little rio all the way to Salizada Pignater. *Molto costoso,* but he had no choice.

Home at last, Sam hoisted his burden up two flights of stairs, thumping it down on every step. At last he was able to slide it across the floor to his study door. Gasping, he unlocked the door, dragged the case inside, and cried out.

The beautiful six-hundred-year-old reliquary from the Scuola di San Giovanni Evangelista lay flat on the table. The small crystal chamber had been shattered. The fragment of the True Cross was gone.

# CHAPTER 27

✂

The most striking thing about Doctor Richard Henchard was not the fact that he was a capable surgeon, educated at the University of London and the Collegio Medico at Bologna. The dominating thing about him was his appearance. If women didn't exactly faint in his presence, they found him irresistible. Sensible grandmothers lost their dignity, middle-aged women made fools of themselves, young women fell all over him.

The poor man couldn't help having an endless series of extra-marital affairs. It could hardly be called his fault. What could a man do if women perpetually surrounded him in billowing clouds, with the fatty muscles clothing their femurs exposed to the great trochanter, their chubby glutei maximi swaying, their globular mammary glands brushing his chest?

Actually Henchard wasn't especially interested in women except as a sort of useful subspecies. You could hardly call them human. Of course he was married to Vittoria, because everybody had a wife, and now he was stuck with that *stupida ragazza* Giovanna, because he couldn't get rid of her, she was always threatening to tell Vittoria. The new place he had found for Giovanna was far too expensive for a mere slut, but naturally he couldn't let her move into the first one on the Rio della Sensa because of the fortune hidden in the closet.

No, women were a bore. What truly engaged Henchard's interest was his medical practice. The patients who came to his office in the Ospedale Civile suffered from fascinating melanomas and other malignancies, and occasionally he ran across a truly remarkable metastatic sarcoma. How could a mere female compare?

And yet the American woman was different. Henchard was captivated by her majestic attractiveness, her clear-eyed calm. He had never known a woman like Mary Kelly. At first he had thought of her as a promising fish, one to be caught with only the most delicate tugs on the line, but now he was letting the line run free. He could see only a day ahead. The quest was thrilling, but it called for patience, for a sedate and old-fashioned kind of wooing. This woman was not about to be fucked against a wall.

But somehow, and sooner rather than later, he would net his fish.

On the day the golden reliquary from the Scuola di San Giovanni Evangelista arrived under guard at Sam Bell's house in the *sestiere* of Castello, Richard Henchard walked out of his own house on Campo San Salvador near Piazza San Marco with a rolled-up sleeping bag under his arm.

Of course Vittoria was as sharp-eyed as ever. "Riccardo, what are you going to do with that thing?"

"One of the interns is going camping," said Henchard smoothly. He patted her backside and kissed her. *"Ciao, cara."*

She leaned against the doorway, watching him go, helplessly enamored in spite of their furious verbal battles. That strong cleft chin of his, those little wrinkles at the corners of his eyes!

❁

In the apartment where his treasure lay, Henchard put the bedroll down in the corner and undid the padlock on the closet door. He wanted to ogle his treasure.

Thank Christ he had come along in time to witness the foolish thievery of that young *spazzino.* Thank God he had seen him standing there with his head through the hole and a gold platter in his hand. The poor *ragazzo* wouldn't have known what to do with it. He would have told his mother and his girlfriend. He might even have gone straight to the editorial offices of *Il Gazzettino*. And then what would have happened? Everybody would have put in their nose.

That bitch in the *agenzia*, Signorina Pastora, she would have fought for the stuff like a cat. The absentee landlord in Milan didn't need the money, but by God he'd put in a powerful claim. And in the end who would get it all, every single thing, every precious piece of Henchard's wonderful discovery? The city of Venice would purloin it as part of its glorious historic heritage. So the wretched *spazzino* would have got nothing. He didn't count.

Nor did Signorina Pastora's client Lorenzo Costanza, Henchard's competitor for possession of the treasure, the fool who had wanted the apartment for his elegant girlfriend. He didn't count either, not anymore. He had been taken care of, and the blame had fallen on his wife. It had been a stroke of luck, the discovery of the weapon in the drawer with her underwear, the little nine-millimeter handgun that was so exactly like his own.

Signora Costanza had run away. Her husband was gone. The *spazzino* was gone. Henchard's treasure was safe.

He knelt within the open door of the closet and looked at the magnificent painting and the gold plates and candlesticks and the odd little castles with their tiny doors. Very carefully he unrolled one of the scrolls. The parchment was covered with handwritten words in another language. What was it? Greek? Hebrew?

Hebrew, that was it. Henchard remembered now. The scrolls were Torah scrolls, inscribed with the first five books of the Bible.

At last, tired of squatting on his knees, he stood up and felt for the padlock, his attention diverted by a new question—

What Jew had put them there?

There was a commotion on the *fondamenta* below. Quickly Henchard strode across the room, slammed the door to the stairway, and threw the bolt across. Only then did he look out the window.

It was only the same crew of men who had been shoveling mud out of the canal for weeks. They were yanking out the corrugated iron barriers at both ends. There were shrieks of metal on metal, shouts and curses. One of the men hopped up and down and flapped his hand. Blood flew. Henchard watched until the man stopped hopping and guffawed and wiped his hand on his shirt. He was all right.

The others kept jerking on the barriers. Water began flowing into the drained canal, rushing faster and faster through the gaps in seething waterfalls. At last one of the men pulled out the last of the metal plates and lifted it over his head with a triumphant shout.

Amused, Henchard left the apartment, forgetting to snap the hasp of the padlock into the staple on the frame of the closet door.

✂

*S*am had been telling himself once again that it didn't matter what happened to him anymore. Why didn't he say farewell to all care and just walk away from the library? Why didn't he abandon his unhappy little daughter and his impossible mother-in-law and fly off to Monte Carlo, or Madrid, or Buenos Aires, or the South Pole? Or perhaps the North Pole? Was the North Pole more congenial than the South Pole? Or why didn't he race across to the mainland and hire a cab and tell the driver to set off at once and find Dottoressa Lucia Costanza? *Subito! Immediatamente!*

But it wasn't working, this cavalier way of thinking. He didn't want to gamble for high stakes in a casino at Monte Carlo. Nor did he want to do any other crazy thing. And there was no omniscient limousine driver in the world who could say, *"Sì, signore,"* and rev up his engine and take off in the right direction to find the missing dottoressa.

No, there was nothing to do but go on with what he was doing, handling the problems that came up in the library, which were sometimes grievous—since the exhibition some of the Aldine incunabula were suffering from a new infestation of woodworm—and examining the relics loaned to him through the good offices of Father Urbano.

But now, staring at the smashed remains of the vandalized reliquary, Sam felt the last vestiges of his happy-go-lucky unconcern fall away. This disaster could not be shrugged off. There'd be hell to pay for sure.

Despairing, he pulled up a chair to the desk where the reliquary lay and sank his head in his hands. It didn't matter any longer what happened to him, but it did matter what happened to the kindly priest who had entrusted him with all these holy objects. Father Urbano's career as a rising man in the church would come to a crashing halt. He'd never be a monsignor or a cardinal patriarch, he'd never ascend to whatever pinnacle of ambition a healthy middle-aged priest might aspire.

But Sam had four weeks' grace. The reliquary from the Scuola di San Giovanni Evangelista had been loaned to him for a month. Not that it mattered. What good would it do to postpone his awful revelation? The shock and the horrified accusations would be the same.

⊠

At Mrs. Wellesley's firm request, Sam always called his mother-in-law by her first name. Ursula too was supposed to call her grandmother Dorothea, but she never did. She never called her anything.

"The word *grandmother* is so old-fashioned," explained Mrs. Wellesley. But it wasn't really a matter of language, it was simply that she couldn't bear to be thought of as an old lady. Certainly not as *una nonna,* an *Italian* grandmother. If Ursula were to call her *Grandma,* people might think she was no longer a young and vibrant woman.

Dorothea didn't tell herself this in so many words. To Sam her lack of an honest connection with her own brain was the whole trouble. The most boring thing about his exquisitely boring mother-in-law was her everlasting unconscious untruthfulness.

Could it have been Dorothea who had entered his study and committed this vile atrocity? After all, she was even more of an iconoclast than he was himself. She might very well have thought it a cleansing act to destroy this remnant of barbarous superstition. Sam cursed his mother-in-law under his breath, wondering how a woman of such extreme respectability could be so violent.

He knocked on her door and confronted her just as she was picking up her alligator bag to go out. "Dorothea," he said sternly, "have you been in my study?"

She looked at him slyly. There was a slight pause, and then she said, "Of course not. How could I? The door is locked."

He jumped at the truth. "You have a key, don't you? You have a key to that room."

"Well, of course I don't have a key. How can you accuse me of such a thing, your own mother-in-law?"

"Because *somebody* opened that door." Sam was so angry he didn't care what he said. "How do I know it wasn't you?"

It was no use. Dorothea Wellesley had an ace in the hole, and it was better than the ace of clubs, the ace of diamonds, the ace of hearts, or the ace of spaces. It trumped every other card in the deck. It was the ace of gold. She simply had a fit.

Sam had seen her fits before. The scene—Dorothea Wellesley having a fit—was familiar and deadly dull. He watched as she threw herself on her bed and gasped between sobs, "How can you say a thing like that to me, *me,* the mother of your own dead wife, *whom you drove into the grave?*"

Frustrated, Sam waited. At last he said loudly over the noisy gulping floods of tears, "Well, have there been any strangers in the house? Could someone else have broken in?"

The tears stopped at once. His mother-in-law sat up, sniffling, and said craftily, "Yes. A plumber. There was a plumber here, fixing the sink."

"Which sink?"

"The kitchen sink. It was plugged up."

Oh, of course, thought Sam, it would be a plumber. There was always a plumber. "You called him? What company was it?"

"Oh, I don't know. I didn't pay much attention. He was in the phone book."

Without a word Sam turned away to find the *Pagine Gialle* and brought it back into her room. He stood over her, flipping the pages, and asked a clever question. "What did you look under? How did you find the list of plumbers in the phone book?"

He had played his ace. Dorothea Wellesley knew little Italian, although she had been married to an Italian and had lived here for years. Sam knew she could never have found a plumber under the word *Idraulici*.

But his ace, as usual, was only the ace of spades. Hers was the usual stupefying ace of gold. Flopping back on the sofa, she began to howl.

✂

*H*omer Kelly sat in the Rare Book Room on the ground floor of the Marciana, where precious books could be examined by serious scholars. He had been given the freedom of this room with the benevolent permission of his friend Samuele Bell, although serious purpose had he none.

It was like a vacation in the South Seas. The overhead lights were the tropical sun, the librarians grass-skirted dancers, the books themselves a feast of roast pig and pineapple. Utterly vanished was the New England landscape that Homer cherished in Concord, the woods and fields of Henry Thoreau, the cold skies that had dropped such transcendental eloquence on the head of Ralph Waldo Emerson.

All that was far away and—could it be?—a little pinched and dry, compared to the wreathed and garlanded riches of the Italian Renaissance. Homer could almost taste the humanist greed of Cardinal Bessarion as he called for the manufacture of yet another codex in Latin or Greek, another Aristotle or Saint Jerome.

Well, it was heaven. Whenever Homer's eyes began to close and he drooped over a beautiful vellum page, he could walk outside to the arcade to watch people threading their way on wooden planks across the pond that was the Piazzetta. Or he could gaze at the staggering view of the lagoon, with San Giorgio Maggiore emerging from the sea like a temple in a dream, and there below the Molo the massed gondolas and the lumbering vaporetti.

This morning he saw a wedding gondola spread with a

golden cloth, the bride's dress foaming out of the fairy vessel like a flower.

"The embarkation for Cythera," murmured Homer, going back indoors, enchanted, unconscious of Sam Bell's wistful dream about a pink-sailed cockleshell that would bear him away to a Cytherean bower with the missing procurator of San Marco, Lucia Constanza.

*"Cosa?"* said the librarian.

*"Niente. Mi scusi,"* whispered Homer, going back to his place at the table.

Today he was bowed over a volume containing the first five books of the Bible. Was it in Hebrew? There were three columns, each in a different hand, all of them hard to decipher.

When Sam touched his shoulder, Homer looked up blindly and said, "I don't understand this at all. Is it Hebrew?"

Sam glanced at the open page and murmured, "The Pentateuch. It's in three languages, Greek, Latin, and Hebrew. It's the first five books of the Bible, bound backward like a Hebrew Torah. Deuteronomy comes first, Genesis last." Sam grasped Homer's coat sleeve and hissed in his ear, "Listen to me, Homer. Can you put this aside for now?"

Homer came to his senses and saw his friend's face clearly. At once he pushed back his chair and whispered, "What's the matter?" Together they went outside and walked along the arcade in a flood of French teenagers. *"Allons y!"* cried the tour guide, holding aloft her umbrella and waving her charges out onto a path of planks leading to San Marco. Some of them merely stepped down into the water, shrieking with laughter.

The tide was ebbing. The next high water was ten hours away. Homer was starving. "What about lunch?" he said. "But, good God, not here."

"No, of course not here," said Sam, and they swept past the little tables of Florian's, where last week Homer had paid six dollars for a cup of cappuccino.

There's a good place across the Rialto Bridge," said Sam. "We'll be there in ten minutes."

⌘

To Homer Kelly, Dottor Samuele Bell was half an enigma. He understood the Bell part all right, the American part, but the Italian part was beyond his grasp. It was clear that Sam was contemptuous of fools. Was that an Italian quality? If so, there was nothing wrong with it. Someone had once told Homer that Italians were a melancholy race—jolly on the surface but gloomy within. Like most generalizations it was probably a lot of bull.

Together they walked quickly to the Rialto Bridge. Halfway up the long staircase Sam stopped to rest, and they leaned over the stone railing and looked down. Below them on the Grand Canal there was a traffic jam. A grubby working boat with a hydraulic lift was crowding a neatly painted craft heading for the Hotel Gritti with a delectable freight of shellfish and fruit. There were cries of *Attenzione!* A crate of grapes tipped into the water. The man at the tiller shouted obscenities, *Vaffanculo! Porca puttana!* and a fishing boat loaded with mussels swerved away in a wide arc.

They turned away from the spectacle and kept on climbing. At the crest of the bridge Homer wondered if he himself had two sides like Sam. It was true that his famous cheerfulness was sometimes only a skim over misery, but usually a healthy optimism prevailed.

"Whoops!" Homer apologized for cannoning into an American girl who had stopped cold in front of him to look at a guidebook, and then he hurried after Sam past the fruit and vegetable stands in the narrow street below the bridge. Beyond the blackberries and grapes he could smell the rich aroma of the fish market, and catch a glimpse of men scooping ice over heaps of calamari and eels, and hear the hoarse cry of *Gamberetti! Cozze! Scampi!*

"Sam, wait for me!" shouted Homer, but he was wedged against a counter of glass baubles from the island of Murano. Nobody was buying glass goldfish. Homer was amused to see the young proprietor talking loudly into a cell phone.

"Hey, look at that kid!" shouted Homer, trying to catch up with Sam. "Those little phones are everywhere."

"I know," said Sam, looking back. "Everybody wants to—what do you call it?—show off with a *telefonino*." He was trying to lead the way into a broad intersection, but it was almost impossible to squeeze through crowds of tourists buying carnival masks like suns and moons and funny hats with checkers and stripes.

Homer shuffled after him, looking at the greedy smiling faces of his American compatriots, wondering if callow cheerfulness was a general American trait. If so, then he was ashamed for his fellow citizens and ashamed for himself. In the face of the troubles of the world, surely cheerfulness was an infantile attitude.

But in the crowded interior of the Cantina do Spade cheerfulness prevailed. Sam and Homer settled down at a small table and Homer looked eagerly at the menu.

Sam was not interested in food. He began talking quickly, leaning forward across the table, his face a mask of misery, and at once Homer was confronted with the enigmatically Italian part of Samuele Bell. He listened with horrified sympathy as Sam told him about the smashed reliquary.

"All I want is to get the relic back," said Sam. "The broken crystal can be repaired. I know a craftsman who can do it. But I can't just whittle another piece of wood to replace the relic that the Scuola has been so proud of for the last five hundred years."

Homer tried to focus his attention on Sam's problem, but he couldn't help looking around and taking pleasure in his surroundings. Dreamily he said, "Byron is supposed to have liked this place."

Sam said despairingly, "Think of the impossibility of finding a few chips of wood in this labyrinth of a city. Probably they've been thrown in the trash already, or dropped into a canal."

Homer tried to sound hopeful. "What if somebody stole them as miracle-working pieces of the True Cross? Is there a marketplace for relics? A dealer in miracles? Hey, you're not eating your lunch. Drink up your wine."

Sam smiled. "Sorry, Homer." He stirred the pasta on his plate. "And there's another thing."

Homer wound fettuccine around his fork and said, "Another thing?"

"Dottoressa Costanza is still missing and the polizia aren't getting anywhere. The carabinieri haven't found her either."

"Dottoressa Costanza? Oh, you mean that woman who killed her husband? The one who ran away with a priceless work of art?"

Sam's fork clattered to the floor. "She didn't kill her husband. That's a lie."

"Well, okay." Homer looked at Sam apologetically and blundered on. "I read in the paper that the murder weapon was covered with her fingerprints. And she obviously packed up in a hurry because her suitcases were missing and half her clothes were scattered all over the floor. And—you'll admit, Sam, that this is pretty damning—she took all her savings out of the bank on the day before his death. And, look here, why would she run away if she didn't do it?"

Sam stared sullenly at his plate. "I don't know, I just know she didn't." He looked up fiercely at Homer. "And she didn't take that little seventeenth-century bronze piece either."

"What makes you think that?"

Sam thumped his fist on the table. "It was that bastard Bernardi, her so-called assistant. When she disappeared, he saw his chance."

"Oh, yes, I remember." Homer laughed. "You told me about him. He's a charter member of your two societies. Both a bore and a bastard, right, Sam? Well, bully for him."

# CHAPTER 30

✄

"Signora!" The proprietor of the *tabacchi* on the corner of Salizada del Pignater was hailing her, leaning out of his shop door. Outside the bar the men of the neighborhood were gathered in a convivial cluster, drinking and smoking. In the bakery the window was full of fancy flat cakes for Saint Martin's Day—Saint Martin and his horse were covered with gumdrops.

Mary stopped, and said, *"Sì?"*

*"Le vostre foto sono pronte."*

*"Bene! Grazie, signore."*

Mary paid for her fat packets of prints and dropped them in her canvas bag. She didn't have time to look at them now. She was on her way to the vaporetto stop on the Riva to meet Richard Visconti. They were planning to spend the day in Murano. After watching a demonstration of glassblowing in the morning, they would look for a place to have lunch. This time she would insist on paying for her own meal.

Of course when the time came, Richard wouldn't hear of such a thing. And then to her embarrassment he bought her a pair of handblown earrings in one of the shops. Most of the things on sale were large and hideous glass objects, but the earrings were lovely twisted bobbles of blown glass. She put them on at once.

He looked at her and then said quietly, *"Bellissima,"* and with a simple gesture took her hand.

It would have been ungrateful to pull it away. And besides— Mary didn't say this to herself, but it was true—she liked his warm clasp, and the sense of something velvety and gentle in the air around them, moving with them as they walked back to the vaporetto stop.

When they disembarked on the Riva degli Schiavoni, she murmured good-bye and walked quickly away, feeling his gaze upon her back. As soon as she turned into the narrow Calle del Dose, she pulled off the earrings and dropped them in her bag.

Homer greeted her with a complaint. "Where were you? You've been gone all day."

"I went to Murano," said Mary. "You know, the place where they blow glass. You take a vaporetto, and there you are. It was *terribly* interesting, Homer. Oh, and look." She rummaged in her bag and brought out her packets of prints. "I haven't looked at them yet."

She was disappointed. They weren't very good. "It's my cheap camera. It must have a really bad lens."

"They look all right to me," said Homer, riffling through one of the packets. He stopped and plucked out a picture. "Who's this?"

"Who do you mean?" Mary looked at it and winced. She had forgotten the picture she had taken of Richard last week in front of a pretty bridge in San Polo. "Oh, I don't know. I strike up conversations with locals all the time."

"This one seems to be carrying your jacket." Homer gave her a questioning look. "And isn't that your bag?"

"Well, of course. He was holding them for me. You know, while I took his picture."

Homer looked at her gravely. "Ah, I see."

Later, running through the pictures again by herself, trying to label them on the back, she couldn't remember what half of them were. Shuffling through them quickly, she mixed up the first batch with the fifth, and the fourth with the second. When she came upon Richard's picture again, she looked at it for a long time, feeling a quickening of her pulse. She had always been impervious to the handsomeness of film stars, but Richard's face was something else again. *Oh, those little crinkles at the corners of his eyes.*

For the first time Mary felt a twinge of shame. She was aware that her feeling for Richard Visconti was beginning to rage out of control. Removing his photograph from the rest, she slipped it between a couple of heavy sweaters in the bottom drawer of her dresser.

Then she spread out the other pictures on the bed and made a selection. The rejected ones she put away, along with the negatives. Afterward she couldn't find them. She remembered exactly where Richard's picture was because she kept taking it out and putting it back, but she couldn't remember where to find the fuzzy picture of a shop window somewhere in San Polo or a miscellaneous bridge that might be anywhere or a random palace somewhere along the Grand Canal.

Her pictures were not sharp and the colors were poor, but Ursula liked them. She leaned against Mary and beamed at the glossy photograph of pigeons eating from her hand in Piazza San Marco.

Her grandmother flipped through them quickly, looking for the picture of herself. "It isn't here," she said, disappointed.

"Oh, there are more." Mary went to look for her second-best collection. Again she couldn't find it. She couldn't find the negatives. Where the hell were they? "I'm sorry, Dorothea," she said, coming back empty-handed. "I'll take another right now if you like."

Mrs. Wellesley went off to arrange her hair, and Mary showed Ursula an out-of-focus shot of a church blanketed in white marble statuary. "Do you know which one this is? I've got them all mixed up." Ursula shook her head. "Oh, well, I'll ask your father. He'll know right away."

# CHAPTER 31

✖

Next day Homer told Mary in confidence about Sam's ghastly trouble—the theft of a couple of relics and the smashing of the borrowed reliquary. "The poor man doesn't know what to do. He's beside himself."

"Well, no wonder. How terrible! Who could have done such a thing?"

"Who knows? Somebody must have a key." Homer sank his voice to a whisper. "Sam suspects his mother-in-law. She's Savonarola in reverse."

"You mean—?"

"Instead of burning vanities like fancy clothes and jewelry, she'd like to burn the Bible."

"I see." Mary laughed. "Look, why don't we take him out to dinner? I'll bring along my pictures, and he can tell me which is which."

Every day the high water was worse. The meteorologist reporting for the local TV station in the Palazzo Labia talked excitedly about the dire results of bureaucratic delay in dealing with *acqua alta*. "One!"—he held up his left hand and raised his fingers one at a time—"the delay in raising the level of the pavement in Piazza San Marco. Two! the delay in constructing mobile barriers and reinforcing the jetties at the three entrances to the lagoon. Three! the delay in completing the dredging of silt from the canals to speed up the flushing of high water. Four! the delay in preventing pollution from the passage of tankers within the island barrier. Five! the delay in preventing the discharge of pollutants from the mainland." The meteorologist gave up on his fingers as a large map appeared behind him. It was alive with arrows running northward in the Adriatic, pointing directly at the city of Venice. The arrows were the violent winds resulting from a steep drop in atmospheric pressure.

The wind was real. Homer, Mary, and Sam were blown sideways as they splashed to the San Zaccaria stop on the Riva through a retreating slop of water, and took the next vaporetto up the Grand Canal. At Ca' Rezzonico there was a famous restaurant with a garden. They sat under a leafy trellis and ordered what Sam recommended, *malfatti alla panna* and *scampi fritti*. Sam himself ordered a plate of squid cooked in its own black ink.

While they were waiting, Mary took out her photographs. "Oh, Sam, forgive me, these are just typical tourist pictures, but perhaps you can identify the ones I can't remember. This one, for instance." She shoved a photograph of an imposing doorway under his nose.

Sam gave it a glance while the waiter set down their plates, and then he snatched it up and looked at it again. "What's this?"

"I don't know." Mary took it from him and showed it to Homer. "That's why I'm asking you. It's a church somewhere, but I don't know which one. Do you know, Homer?"

"God, how should I know?" said Homer, who was still steeped in ignorance, except of course about the Aldine *Dream of Poliphilius* and the illuminated *Vitruvius* of Cardinal Bessarion, and other ancient works.

Sam took the picture back and said softly, "It's Lucia. I swear it's Lucia."

"Lucia?"

"This woman walking in front of the church. It's Lucia Costanza. The new procurator of San Marco. You remember, Homer. I told you about her."

"Oh, right," said Homer, taking an interest at once. "I read about her in the *New York Times* before we came. She's the one who's supposed to have killed her husband, only you swear she didn't."

"Because she disappeared," exclaimed Mary, putting two and two together. "Isn't she the woman the carabinieri are looking for? The one who vanished when her husband was murdered?"

Sam gazed at Mary's picture. "She's alive, she's here. She's somewhere here in Venice." He threw back his napkin and stood up. "When was this? When did you take this picture? Where were you?"

"Oh, Sam, I'm terribly sorry. I haven't the faintest idea where I was."

Sam pawed at the back of his chair and pulled on his coat. "I'll look for it. I'll look until I find it."

Mary groped under the table for her bag. "Books, Sam, we can look for it in books. I've got a really good guidebook. It's chock-full of churches."

"You mean we're leaving?" Homer looked with dismay at his dinner, for which he was about to pay forty thousand lire.

In a far corner of the same restaurant Doctor Richard Henchard was having dinner. Turning his head, he saw Mary Kelly in the company of two men. One was familiar to him. At once he shifted his chair behind the trunk of a climbing vine. Turning up the collar of his jacket, he shivered and said to his dinner partner, *"Ho freddo. E lei? Non trova che faccia un po' freddo?"*

The pretty nurse with whom he was dining was new in his surgery, a clumsy girl with a habit of dropping instruments into abdominal cavities. In answer to his question she shook her head and went on with her story about the Virgin's veil.

"Haven't you heard? It's so exciting. They've found a piece of the blue veil of the Virgin Mary. It's on display in the Church of Santo Spirito. Of course"—the nurse didn't want to seem old-fashioned, because, after all, Riccardo was a scientist—"one doesn't know whether to believe it or not, but they say it's already cured a crippled child." The nurse gazed at Henchard worshipfully. "What do you think, Riccardo?" Oh, God, he had such magnificent eyes, with the most adorable little wrinkles at the corners. In addressing her he was still using the formal "lei." The pretty nurse hoped for an impassioned "tu" before the evening was over.

She hoped in vain. Henchard had another conquest in mind. Not tonight, but soon, very soon.

# CHAPTER 32

✂

They couldn't find it, the place where Lucia Costanza was striding so purposefully across Mary's photograph from right to left. The church facade in the background refused to be identified.

Mary looked for it in her guidebooks. Sam ransacked his shelves for textbooks on Venetian architecture. He borrowed Dorothea's big coffee-table book, *Venice, City of Enchantment*, which was packed with huge color photographs of the Ducal Palace, San Marco, the crowds in the piazza, gondolas against the sunset, the masked revelers of carnival time, the costumed rowers of the Regata Storica. The church they were looking for was not to be found.

Next day Sam fell ill. He set out early in the morning two hours before his first appointment in the Marciana to look at obscure churches in the unvisited neighborhood north of the public gardens. It was one of the many places where Mary had lost her way.

"I took pictures just the same," she told Sam, "even when I didn't know where I was. I wandered all over the place in Sant' Elena beyond the Giardini, and I was really mixed up between the Zattere and the Rio Nuovo."

The *sestiere* called Sant' Elena was one of the higher regions of the city. There was little evidence of high water, but before Sam had been out of the house five minutes on his way along the Riva to the Giardini, he felt so faint he had to turn around and go back.

He locked himself in his study, dropped heavily on the bed,

and turned his face away from the sight of the vandalized reliquary on the table.

At once the usual scene began to play in his head. *A courtyard with statuary, a staircase, a woman on the stairs, an office, a window overlooking another courtyard, the woman walking quickly in front of him and sitting down, his own hands on her desk, his voice and her laughter. Where was she?*

᠅

She was not far away. Dottoressa Lucia Costanza had not fled to the mainland to conceal herself somewhere in the Veneto. It had never occurred to Lucia to lose herself in some crowded metropolis like New York or London or even in the city of Rome. She was serenely convinced that the crime of her husband's murder would sooner or later be solved, and then she could come out of hiding and reorganize her life and resume her interrupted career.

Her attempt at renting an apartment, that simple little place near the Casa del Tintoretto, had been cut short by the man who had turned up on the doorstep claiming to have an earlier lease.

The apartment hadn't been worth fighting for anyway. It was dingy, and serious repairs would have been required to fix the closet wall. Lucia had given up at once, deciding to take a chance on the loan of a place in Cannaregio belonging to an old school friend, now working in America. She had nearly forgotten the key the friend had thrust upon her, but now she extracted it gratefully from her bag and settled in.

She had begun to recover from the fearful shock of learning from newspaper headlines that her poor unhappy husband had been killed and that she herself was under suspicion. At first she couldn't believe it. Leaving Lorenzo Costanza had been such an ordinary thing, painful but ordinary, the long-overdue act of a perfectly ordinary aggrieved wife. And it hadn't been easy. It had taken courage to abandon her home and begin a new life. It had been like amputating a diseased part of her body in order to save the rest. She had felt lopped and chopped.

That had been bad enough, but the rest was a nightmare. Poor Lorenzo was dead! Of course she had long since lost all respect for her husband, but she would not have wished his life to be so violently cut short. And she couldn't get used to the fact that she was now the object of *una caccia all' uomo,* a manhunt. It sickened Lucia to read the details of the lurid case against her. *"The old, old story! SHE was ambitious, HE was a man with a poetic nature."* If the revelations in the paper hadn't been so persuasive and threatening, she would have laughed.

She was grateful that the only picture they had found was a snapshot of a solemn thirteen-year-old with braces on her teeth, taken long ago at the school of the Suore Canossiane in Murano. It had been taken under duress—

> *"Ma, cara Lucia, tutti devono avere una fotografia!"*
> *"O, Suora, non io, per favore!"*

But of course they had insisted. After that, she had always resisted and refused and ducked her head and turned her back, and destroyed any pictures that turned up, because in photographs she always looked so ugly. Her nose looked even bigger than it was, and her neck too long and thin.

So the image of the gawky pigtailed kid with braces on her teeth was the only one left. It looked ridiculous next to the story about some terrible woman who had killed her husband and run away. But it wasn't funny, not really. The hideously incriminating account had appeared not only in the local papers but in the national dailies, *Corriere della Sera* and *La Repubblica*. It meant walking away from her splendid new position as a procurator of San Marco, it meant unpinning her thick, too-curly hair and letting it fall around her face, it meant hiding herself away in this small square and becoming a person known as Signora Sofia Alberti.

But it was all right. Lucia liked the neighbors and she liked the square. Every day she shopped in the *alimentari* of young Stefano, who teased her—*"Signora Sofia Alberti? No, no! Sofia*

*Loren!*" For fresh fruits and vegetables there was a little *negozio* presided over by a kindly old woman. "*Questa, cara mia?*" she would say, picking out the finest head of lettuce, chattering about her grandchildren as she twisted the corners of the wrapping paper. In the square Lucia admired the fat babies and chatted with their mothers. She knew the names of all the little boys riding tricycles and bouncing footballs against the trees in the middle of the square.

Sometimes she held one end of a skipping rope while a grandmother held the other for two little girls who jumped and tangled their feet and hopped happily up and down. She showed them how to skip in a dancing step, right foot forward, left foot back.

She taught them to make paper boats like cocked hats, and drop them from one side of the bridge over the Rio de la Misericordia. "You see? It's like a race. They float under the bridge and come out on the other side, so if every boat has a name, you'll know who wins."

They were overjoyed. They scribbled their names with crayon. "Yes, yes," cried Guido, "look at mine!"

"*Anna*, mine's *Anna*!"

"Look, look, mine's *Regina*!"

"Oh, signora, write your name too! Your boat will be *Sofia*!"

But it wasn't. When she wrote LUCIA on the side of her paper boat, they were puzzled for a minute, but then at once they began fighting over Guido's boat, which had won unfairly because he sank Regina's with a stone.

She would be patient. Lucia was an optimist. The world had not come to an end. Eventually things would straighten themselves out.

In the meantime, while she waited for something to happen, there was nothing to do. There was a tedious sameness to every day. With her wraparound dark glasses and loose hair, she felt disguised enough to walk as far as the Strada Nuova for a newspaper, careful to choose times of day when the rising water was not a problem.

She didn't dare go farther. She didn't dare show herself in public places where she might run into people she knew.

Longingly Lucia read the notice in *Il Gazzettino* about a concert in the great monastic Church of Santa Maria Gloriosa dei Frari. A chorus and soloists from the Conservatory of Padua were to be accompanied by the local Orchestra di Venezia, musicians decked out in eighteenth-century costume.

She wished she could go. She wanted to hear arias and choruses from one of Monteverdi's Venetian operas and from oratorios by Handel and Hayden. There would even be a sumptuous chorus from Bach's *Saint Matthew Passion*.

On the night of the concert Lucia went to bed early. As soon as she closed her eyes a fragmentary vision from last month came back without her bidding, the day when that crazy man had walked into her office with his two ridiculous proposals. Like a constantly rewound piece of tape, the vision appeared and reappeared.

He would walk in and put his hands on her desk and say that insane thing, and then a moment later, after the tape had rewound itself, he would walk in just as gallantly and say it again. And then again.

H omer Kelly had nothing against music. In fact he liked music, on the whole. And he had heard some of this music before.

How could he ever forget the performance of Handel's *Messiah* in Harvard's Memorial Hall, with its wild interruption? Of course it had been Bach's *Saint John Passion*, not the *Saint Matthew*, that he had heard with Mary in the Church of the Commonwealth in Boston, but that event had been insane too, because the entire audience had narrowly escaped being crushed to death by a collapsing vault. In Homer's experience exalted music was often accompanied by staggering climaxes of catastrophe or joy.

But there were no astonishing interruptions this evening in the enormous spaces of the monastic Church of Santa Maria Gloriosa dei Frari during the performance of selections from the sacred music of Hayden and Handel, Monteverdi and Bach. The lofty vaults stayed put. No long-dead ghost appeared beyond the rood screen to bring the entire audience to its feet, to topple the bass viols and entangle the music stands of the second violins. Tonight the several parts of the program followed one another serenely.

Sam Bell sat with Mary and Homer on folding chairs between the old choir stalls, listening, staring up at the same time at the painting over the altar, Titian's *Assumption of the Virgin*. Buoyed up on clouds and supported by the thrust of the springy bellies of her attendant cherubs, she seemed to be lifting her hands in wonder at the chorus from the *Saint Matthew Passion*.

It was the wild mob scene near the end, with all the citizens of Jerusalem shouting at Pilate, *"Lass ihn kreuzigen, lass ihn kreuzigen."*

Homer stuck his elbow into Sam's side, and muttered, "What the hell are they saying?"

"Ssshhh, Homer," whispered Mary.

Sam gave Homer a bitter sidelong glance and translated softly, *"Let him be crucified."*

"Oh," said Homer, and for a moment he kept still, but when the chorus shouted something else, *"Sein Blut komme über uns und unsere Kinder,"* he nudged Sam again. "Blood, what's that they're singing about blood?"

Sam muttered it under his breath, "His blood be on us and on our children. Shut up, Homer."

"Oh, right."

*"Please!"* Someone was leaning forward from the row of seats behind them, hissing in Homer's ear, "Would you kindly pipe down? *Some* of us are trying to hear the *music.*"

It was the bishop of Seven Oaks, acting as spokesman for his delegation of music lovers from the British Isles.

Homer squirmed around and saw the four glowering British faces, and perceived at once that he had been a boor. "Oh, sorry, sorry." He hunched his head apologetically down into his shoulders and turned back to the chorus.

But the shouting had stopped. For a moment the high vaults rang with the echo—*Kinder, Kinder*—and then the fiddlers and flutists lowered their instruments and mopped their brows and the singers filed out. It was all over.

Gasping, emotionally frazzled, Mary and Homer staggered out of their seats and wandered around the huge church, while Sam guided them to more masterpieces of Venetian painting. They could hardly take them in. They were suffering from something they had experienced in Florence, aesthetic overload.

Rising against one wall were reliquaries like the ones in the Treasury of Saint Mark, containing miscellaneous holy bits of bone. Sam gave them a contemptuous wave of his arm, and they headed for home.

It was true that there had been no collapse of the high brick vaulting, no astonishing apparition disrupting the music. And yet something alarming and climactic had happened, although Homer was not yet aware of it. A crack had appeared in his mind. Later on it would produce a mighty fall of rock.

# CHAPTER 34

Once again it was raining. In the Hotel Danieli a lavish morning tea was spread before the bishop of Seven Oaks and his lady and the member of Parliament for the Channel Islands and his wife. There were sofas and tapestried chairs, silver teapots and damask napkins, tea wagons with cakes and scones and raspberry jam.

Everything within the hotel was perfectly satisfactory. Outside, it was not. Water slopped over the edge of the lagoon and slipped across the pavement to the very door of the hotel.

The bishop, Arthur Cluff-Luffter, was accustomed to speaking with authority. "You know, we don't have to stay here. There are other hotels in this city."

"But won't the management be angry?" said Louise Alderney, wife of Tertius Alderney, the member of Parliament. "Aren't we committed here to a full week?"

"Oh, we may have to pay an extra day in apology, but it's not like a contract in law."

Then the bishop leaned forward, waving a cupcake. "I know an excellent alternative, the Hotel Flora. Everybody recommends the Flora."

"But is it on higher ground?" said his wife shrewdly. "That's the important thing. It's all that really matters."

The bishop popped the cupcake into his mouth and whipped out a map showing the distribution of high water. He consulted it gravely, changing one pair of spectacles for another. Then he folded the map and shook his head. "Sorry, chaps, it won't do. It's an island surrounded by water."

"Our big mistake was the decision to come in November," said the MP, frowning at the bishop, who had been at fault.

"Oh, it doesn't really matter," said Elizabeth Cluff-Luffter generously, throwing herself back in her chair. "I can write my novel anywhere. It's all in my head."

"But, Elizabeth," said Louise Alderney, "they say the water is rising every day. It's going to get worse and worse. Perhaps we should all go home."

"Nonsense, Louise," said Elizabeth. "Where's your fighting spirit? Don't be so timid." She raised her fist in a gallant gesture. "Let us splash on."

"Oh, if only I'd brought my wellies," said Louise.

⁂

The Piazza Council was not as accepting of the current state of *acqua alta* in the city of Venice as was Elizabeth Cluff-Luffter. At their second urgent meeting in the Hall of the Council of Ten, three more members of the Consorzio Venezia Nuova showed up. They sat together at one end of the table and complained loudly about their bad press, when of course everyone knew perfectly well that the delay in the construction of the mobile barriers in the lagoon was not their fault at all, it was the fault of the City Council.

Angry looks were directed at the other end of the table, where the mayor sat between Sam Bell and Acting Procurator Tommaso Bernardi. Behind the mayor a door opened on the staircase where wretched citizens accused by the Council of Ten had once been led away to prison cells. Obviously the Consorzio Venezia Nuova would have liked to enjoy the same condemnatory power.

They glowered at the mayor and one of them spoke his mind. "It is the City Council which has prevented the construction of the floodgates at the ports of Lido, Malamocco, and Chioggia. Our hydraulic model at Voltabarozzo has been proven to work. When can we expect the permission and the funding to begin in earnest?"

"Unfortunately," growled the mayor, "your hydraulic model does not take into account all the complexities of the situation."

It was a typical long-standing argument. Sam broke in to plead for practical temporary measures to protect the piazza right now, because, after all, it was no joke. When the worst of the high water came rushing into the square, there would be injury to the foundations of their grand historic buildings and flooding of their ground floors, accompanied by all the bad effects of moisture on walls and ceilings and precious works of art, including the rare old books in the Biblioteca Marciana.

"At least we can be grateful that there are fewer tourists at this time of year," said Father Urbano, thinking of his summertime nightmare, the endless lines of people shuttling through the basilica. "It's amazing that these latecomers are willing to walk on the platforms and wait their turn to come in, even in heavy rain."

"Well, you can't blame them," said the superintendent of Venetian fine arts and history. "They've flown halfway around the world, and by God they're going to see everything they've been promised."

"And of course everything they've been promised," said Sam sarcastically, "is in our part of the city. Which just happens to be at one of the lowest points in Venice. Why don't the tourist agencies tell them about other attractions—the Scuola di San Rocco, for instance, and the Naval Museum?"

Another official body was represented at the meeting, L'Ufficio Idrografico del Magistrato alle Acque. "We will of course," promised their spokesman, "send our usual daily faxes forecasting the heights and times of *acqua alta.*"

Gloom prevailed. On the way into the building they had all experienced the results of the rising water. They had threaded their way into the meeting through masses of tourists mincing along the duckboards into San Marco and the Ducal Palace, and through the throngs crowding the arcades of the Procuratie Vecchie, the Procuratie Nuove, the Museo Correr, and the Libreria di Sansovino.

"One finds it so difficult to get into one's office," complained Signor Bernardi, the delegate from the headquarters of the procurators of San Marco.

*One's office,* thought Sam angrily. It wasn't *one's* office, it was *Lucia's* office.

"Well, anyway," said the dejected mayor, "does anyone have a suggestion for dealing with the coming disaster?"

"I do," said Signor Bernardi, raising a soft white hand. "I suggest we set up blockades at all the entrances to the piazza and allow only a certain number of people in at a time."

Sam was stunned. How fascinating! He had already admitted Bernardi into his private Society of Bastards, but simple admission was surely not enough. Sam stopped listening to the experts and began thinking up hierarchies of honor—Bastards Simple and Complex, Evil and Malevolent, Filthy and Abominable. Which one was right for Bernardi?

Leaving the meeting, Sam was surprised to find that his appetite had come back. He was actually hungry for lunch.

## CHAPTER 35

The siren went off very early, five blasts ten seconds apart. *High water today,* hooted the siren. *Put on your boots!*

Mary had no boots, but she didn't care. She had a date with Richard very early. It was as though they could no longer bear to be apart.

"What's that noise?" said Homer drowsily, lifting his head from the pillow.

"It means high water today," murmured Mary, heading for the shower. Homer went back to sleep.

Before creeping out of the apartment Mary left him a note—*Out all day. Love, M.*

He wouldn't like it, but at least he wouldn't call the police.

Henchard had prepared the way. The apartment on the Rio della Sensa was grubby, but he couldn't very well take Mary Kelly to his own house, and he certainly couldn't use Giovanna's place on Calle de la Madonna, because Vittoria and Giovanna were squatting in them like toads.

He met Mary at the San Marcuola vaporetto stop, welcoming her with a passionate embrace. Then he took her hand and propelled her along the zigzagging streets of Cannaregio, through Campo Santa Fosca, where there was a statue, but Mary didn't ask whose it was, because they were not talking, only walking very quickly, making a left turn, crossing a bridge, a second bridge, a third, a fourth.

Tintoretto's house, thought Mary, stepping off the last bridge into two inches of water. Together they splashed along the *fondamenta* beside the Rio della Sensa. It was no longer a muddy gulf but a full and brimming canal. Richard did not slow down as they passed the house with the sign on the wall—

JAC. ROBUSTI QUI TINTORETTO
DOMUM VETUSTAM

He stopped five or six doors away.

It was where she had first seen him. She had been taking pictures and he had been standing there and she had asked him if Tintoretto's house was open to visitors and he had said no. That was the beginning.

She watched as he fumbled with his key and opened the door. Willingly she followed him up the stairs. They were both overwhelmed.

She saw the room in a haze. Except for a sleeping bag on the floor it was empty. It was an old room with sooty plaster walls. On one side two dirty windows looked out on the canal, on another a bathroom door stood open, and beside it was another door, tightly shut. The second door had no handle, only a dangling padlock.

They fell on their knees on the sleeping bag, and Richard caressed her and undressed her and made love to her tenderly, and then they fell sweetly asleep.

Henchard had netted his fish.

## CHAPTER 36

✂

When she woke up, Richard was no longer beside her. Mary could hear the sound of the shower behind the bathroom door. Then as she looked sleepily at the wall, something like a dream began to happen. The other door drifted silently ajar, and the narrow space beyond it was full of gold.

She sat up, awestruck. Gold-handled scrolls leaned upright in the closet. They were bedecked with golden bells. Gold plates and goblets and candlesticks lay on the floor. There were packages wrapped in newspaper and tied with rotting string. A large painting in a gold frame was propped against the curtain on the back wall of the closet. In her visionary state Mary could see every detail. It was a portrait of a beautiful young man with a fur cloak slung over his shoulder. He had a smiling face and dark eyes that gazed directly into hers. *I see you. I have always seen you. I have known you since time began.*

What were all these things? How had they come here?

She jumped up and pulled on her slip. The shower was still running. She went to the open door of the closet, aware of a faint tinkling sound as her bare feet crossed the floor. Something was weirdly wrong.

Back home in Concord Mary had once cleared out the attic of an ancient cousin, and it had been a strange experience. The boxes of papers and books, the burst trunks, the heaps of memorabilia, all had been covered with a peculiar sort of dirt—

gray sawdust from the insect-ridden beams overhead, crumbled plaster and powdery black specks, as though the passing years themselves had been pounded into moldering fragments and dropped from the sky. The things in this closet on the Rio della Sensa in the city of Venice were like that. The gold gleamed through a coating of dust that was old, very old.

Mary stooped and brushed the debris from the newspaper wrapping on one of the packages that lay on the floor. The yellowed sheet was disintegrating at the edges, but the printed name of the newspaper was clear and black—

### GAZZETTA DI VENEZIA
#### DOMENICA 5 DICEMBRE 1943

*December 1943!* The newspaper was more than half a century old! Mary bent lower and read a fragment of a heading—

> *PRIMO RASTRELLAMENTO . . .*
> *EBREI A VENEZIA. I DEPORTATI . . .*

*Ebrei* meant Jews. She didn't know the meaning of the word *rastrellamento* but it had an ugly sound. *Deportati* could mean only one thing.

She stood up and backed away. Something grim and terrible had saturated all the objects in the closet. It permeated everything—the painting, the candlesticks, the gold plates, the tall scrolls with their dangling bells. It struck her in the face like a foul smell.

The sound of the shower stopped. Mary moved back to the sleeping bag and lay down, thinking hard. When Richard came out of the bathroom he knelt beside her, then gave a great start and sprang up, whispering a furious *"Shit."* Plunging across the room he slammed the door of the closet and rattled the padlock, snapping it shut. Then he came back and stood over Mary, staring down at her, breathing hard.

It was all wrong. Everything had changed. Without a word Mary got to her feet.

Henchard said nothing as she reached for her clothes and carried them into the bathroom. When she came out, fully dressed, he was still standing there, still looking at her, still silent. Mary gathered up her bag. She didn't know how to say good-bye.

Their silence was not like the wordlessness of their earlier panting progress through the streets of Cannaregio, nor like the silence of their rush up the stairs. It was a menacing exchange of unsaid questions and answers—

*What are those things in the closet?*

*I can't say.*

*Where did they come from?*

*I can't tell you.*

When she was gone, clumping down the stairs in her boots, Henchard cursed his own carelessness. How the bloody hell could he have left the padlock unhooked? She had seen it! She had seen everything, because every goddamn thing was right there in full view.

Angrily he stood at the window and watched her walk away, wading slowly through the rising water of the tide that was threatening to be the highest yet. As usual, the goddamn woman was interested in everything. *God, look at her!* She was exchanging greetings with a couple of grinning *muratori* who were wading toward her with picks and shovels. He watched her mount the steps of the bridge and stride across it, glancing back once at his window, her face clear and composed.

Oh, Christ, he shouldn't have let her go! He should have soothed her, he should have overpowered her once again with his ardor, he should have made love to her. And then it would have been so easy to make up a lie about the closet. Almost anything would have been good enough. Instead he had stood there tongue-tied like a fool.

One thing was certain. The things would have to be moved.

She might come back tomorrow, or even today, along with her husband, that big important university professor, and a bunch of goddamn police or carabinieri with handfuls of official documents. Jesus Christ, they'd have a search warrant, *un mandato di perquisizione*. No, no, it mustn't happen. The stuff had to go. It had to go right now.

⌗

*T*o Richard Henchard, watching her cross the bridge over the Rio della Sensa, Mary Kelly looked serenely untroubled. She was not.

Following her nose in the direction of the wide shopping strada beyond Campo Santa Fosca, she thought about her affair with the man who called himself Richard Visconti. On her part there had been no personal will involved, no choice, no moral pondering. It had been like going over Niagara in a barrel. She did not feel guilty, at least not yet.

But a heavy burden of guilt might have been better than this. If she were merely feeling guilty, she could have preened herself on being like some of her trendy friends, women who carried on extramarital affairs in a wild roller coaster of guilt and excitement.

What was unbearable was the knowledge that she, Mary Morgan Kelly, author of seven scholarly books, tenured professor at a famous university, had been such an idiot.

She had to dodge sideways on the Fondamenta della Misericordia to find another bridge. Beyond it two men hoisted bags of trash into a boat. No gondolas were in sight. Mary guessed that Cannaregio was out of the tourist loop. It was a neighborhood for Italians. The election posters were not for tourists— *Per VENEZIA, per MESTRE, per il VENETO, con MASSIMO BARBATO, con MARIO RUSSO.*

She kept going, squelching along in her rubber boots, passing a woman trailing a shopping cart, a cat making its way along a housetop, an old man sweeping the pavement, a young man with a cell phone clamped to his ear, a *panetteria* with fanciful cakes in the window.

Mary stopped to look at the cakes, which were cut in the shape of horsemen and decorated with candies and swags of icing. The horsemen were figures of Saint Martin, because today was Saint Martin's day. She walked on, thankful that this part of the city was dry. It was a relief not to be wading in shallow water.

Here on the Strada Nuova every vestige of her infatuation was gone. She flicked off Richard Visconti like a horse shuddering its skin to get rid of a fly. Suddenly ravenous, she plunged into a bar and sat down solemnly to drink a cappuccino and eat a miniature sandwich, ready at last to think about the golden apparition behind Richard's closet door.

Half the tiny sandwich disappeared in one bite. Mary closed her eyes, trying to remember, making a list in her head. There had been the wonderful painting of the young man with a spotted fur over his shoulder, and on the floor the shapeless packages in their tragic wrappings, and leaning in the corner two or three tall scrolls with golden handles. There had also been a display of glittering cups and plates and tall golden candelabra, the kind with a lot of candles in a single row. How many candles? Seven? Eight? Nine?

Of course, of course. They were Hebrew candlesticks. The scrolls were Torah scrolls. The plates and cups were vessels for the celebration of Passover. The assembled treasure was a kind of Hebrew holy grail. It must have been hidden in that shabby apartment on the Rio della Sensa in 1943, during a time of mortal danger for the Jews of Venice. What did Richard have to do with the fate of Venetian Jews during the Second World War? He had not even been born in 1943.

Mary set down her coffee cup, snatched up her bag, and hurried out of the bar. Whatever it meant, it was infinitely more important than a feverish episode of mindless adultery. It meant something bad, something terrible. In the golden aura streaming out of Richard Visconti's closet there had been something grotesque, something that had swept her out of the room and out of the house, something profoundly awful, something that implicated Richard and dashed him out of all caring—but something unspeakably larger than Richard Visconti.

Outside the bar the street was full of shoppers, the sky was gray. Mary took out her map. It was an old-fashioned map, elaborately folded. She had opened and closed it so many times that the creases were coming apart. Now she batted it open and put her eyes close to the printed network of street names and figured out where to go.

She should follow the Strada to a biggish street called Rio Terrà Farsetti—Rio Terrà meant a filled-in canal—then turn left. Pretty soon there'd be a bridge, and on the other side she would find herself in the Ghetto Nuovo.

The Strada was empty of water, but the streets northwest of it were wet. In boots it didn't matter. She was used to wading. But when she crossed the bridge into the Ghetto Nuovo, she found it perfectly dry.

Of course the square looked familiar. She had been here before, taking pictures. She remembered the sad bronze memorials on the wall, and the trees, and the old wellhead. Mary paused under a tree to empty the water out of her boots.

Somewhere here there was a museum. Yes, there was the sign, MUSEO EBRAICO. Was it open at eleven o'clock in the morning? Yes, it was. She paid her way in.

The exhibition space was on the upper floor. Mary climbed the stairs to a display of Torah scrolls and seven-branched candlesticks and splendid ritual dishes. She was reminded of the pewter communion plates in old New England churches, but these were more elaborate, and they were incised with Hebrew words. And everything was silver, not pewter, and certainly not gold.

It occurred to her that gold, while much more expensive than silver, was more practical in one way. Over the course of years a silver vessel would tarnish and turn black, whereas gold would stay shining forever.

She stood for a long time gazing at the bright silver cups and

Passover plates and the little silver vessels with tiny doors for the dispensing of incense. Someone was keeping them diligently polished. Even so, they were less magnificent than Richard's glorious golden vessels.

But there was a more significant difference. Here there was no sinister aura, no sense of suffering, no terror. It was merely a museum of beautiful sacred objects.

Mary went back downstairs and bought a book in the museum shop, attracted by the picture on the cover. It was a photograph of a crowd of people on a sunny street surrounding a man who was carrying a Torah. All the men were wearing hats, some of the women held babies. It was surely an important occasion. Somehow the picture struck a blow.

Oh, God, she was tired. She wanted to go home.

Which way to the vaporetto stop? Many plodded across another bridge and walked under a sign, GHETTO VECCHIO. It was the wrong way. She had been here before. It was not the way home. This little street led straight back to a synagogue. Last time there had been men going in and out, boys on the doorstep. Today there was no one. The synagogue was closed.

Then, tired as she was, Mary stopped short and gasped with recognition, because it was the church portal in her photograph. It was the one Sam was looking for. When they had pored over pictures of scores of Venetian churches, they had been making a simple mistake. It wasn't a church at all. The imposing building in the background of Mary's accidental photograph of Lucia Costanza was not a Christian church, it was a synagogue.

In the vaporetto on the way home Mary took out the book she had bought in the Museo Ebraico and read the title, *Gli Ebrei a Venezia, 1938–1945*. As the boat chugged around the bend of the Grand Canal she turned the pages, slowly deciphering the Italian words, aware that the answer to the puzzle was beginning to reveal itself. The sense of horror emanating from the golden treasure in Visconti's closet was not a hallucination. The horror was real.

✂

The place where Giovanna had been installed by Riccardo 'Enciard—Giovanna couldn't pronounce his English name—wasn't exactly what she would have liked, a pretty apartment in a place where she could go shopping with her friends. This part of Cannaregio was a long way from any fashionable neighborhood.

The only people on the street were small children, middle-aged women, and laborers taking up the pavement and putting it down again. The only sounds were the harsh scraping of the shovels of the *muratori* and the silly shouts of the children. There were no elegant shops. It was true that Riccardo sometimes gave her expensive presents, but this time he had been *estremamente spilorcio,* really stingy. She had a TV set, but he kept forgetting to arrange for a telephone. How did he expect her to get along without a phone?

"This place is closer to the hospital," that was his excuse. "So I can drop in on you at lunchtime."

But it had been weeks since he had dropped in at all. And yet she was supposed to be there for him at noon every day, just in case! It wasn't fair. It meant that she couldn't spend an entire day with Minetta or go shopping in Mestre with Serena. She couldn't even chat on the phone or arrange a meeting.

Giovanna spent much of her time in bed, wearing one of the pretty nightgowns Riccardo had given her. At first she took a shower every day and powdered and perfumed herself and painted her face and shaved her legs and did her nails and arranged her hair in front of the mirror, just in case he might drop by. But now that he came so seldom it was a waste of time. So Giovanna often didn't bother to get up. She lay in bed, not always very clean, eating sweets and playing solitaire or mending the lace edging on her underwear, while the television screen jiggled and bounced across the room because it was company.

So it was a shock when he suddenly appeared and told her imperiously that she had to move out. "Right now, Giovanna. *Subito!* I've found you another place." His arms were full of lumpy plastic bags.

She reared up in bed. "But, Riccardo!"

"Now! *Ascolta!* I said right now." He set his bags down on the floor, then strode across the room to her wardrobe. "Here, put this on."

"But why?" She got out of bed, reached for the dress, and looked at him slyly. "It's your wife, isn't it? Your wife is coming."

"Yes, yes, my wife. Come on. *Andiamo!*"

On the television screen the commercial for a carpet-cleaning service came to an end and a newswoman appeared, a gorgeous creature with a cascade of golden hair. Briskly she announced the day's headlines. While Giovanna bustled around, Riccardo ran down the stairs again and came back with a clumsy armful wrapped in a tarpaulin. It tinkled and jingled. This too he put down on the floor.

"What's all this stuff?" said Giovanna, fumbling behind her back with her bra.

"It's none of your fucking business."

Giovanna sniffled, and he ran downstairs again. By the time she finished dressing he had made two more trips up and down. The corner of the room was cluttered with mysterious bulky objects in plastic bags—squarish, roundish, and flattish—and a few long objects clumsily wrapped in the tarp.

Giovanna was intensely inquisitive. When Riccardo ran downstairs for the last time she poked under the tarp and saw a glint of gold. Hastily she covered it up as he thundered up the stairs again. "Okay," he said brusquely. *"Avanti!"*

Giovanna couldn't believe it. "But what about my things?"

She waved her arm dramatically at the bed with its cozy comforter and fluffy pillows, her ruffled curtains, her dressing table, the wardrobe full of her clothes, and the chaise on which they had so often made love.

"Later. I'll have everything sent over later. Giovanna, I have an appointment! Come on!"

"But, Riccardo! My television! I can't do without my television set!"

Then for a moment they both turned to look at it. The blond beauty from Rome had vanished, and it was the turn of a ripe peach from Venice to relay the latest information on a Venetian murder investigation. "There has been no movement in the Costanza murder case," said the ripe peach. "The principal suspect, Dottoressa Lucia Costanza, the murdered man's runaway wife, is rumored to be in Vicenza. This snapshot of Dottoressa Costanza is a television first. It was taken last year by her neighbor, Signora Maria Adelberti. If any viewer has seen this woman, please call this station."

And there she was, Dottoressa Lucia Costanza, a handsome woman in an old shirt, trimming a rosebush.

Henchard cried, "Shit! Fucking shit!" and sank down on the bed.

"What is it, Riccardo?" said Giovanna, dumbfounded.

Oh, Christ, it was his own fault. He had seen her, she had been right there on the *fondamenta* beside the apartment on the Rio della Sensa. He had jumped to a conclusion, too fast, too fast! He had assumed she was just somebody's girlfriend. He should have seen at once that a woman with her bearing couldn't possibly be a common whore like Giovanna. Oh, God forgive him, he had made a gruesome mistake.

Henchard ground his teeth and covered his face with his hands, trying to think. He ran his memory back to the day in the *agenzia* with Signorina Pastora. She had turned away from him to talk on the telephone, he remembered that, and he had picked up from her desk the lease signed by the other client, and read the name and address.

Oh, Christ, had it been *S.re L. Costanza,* meaning the husband, Lorenzo Costanza, or *Sig.ra L. Costanza,* meaning the wife, Lucia Costanza? *Fucking Christ,* he had assumed it was the husband! He had matched the whole thing to his own life, to his own rental of the apartment for a girlfriend, his own discovery of the treasure in the closet. He had assumed the wretched Costanza had discovered it. He had assumed that the woman at the door was merely his girlfriend, when she was really his wife.

She was Lucia Costanza herself. It was Lucia Costanza who had tried to rent the apartment because she was leaving her husband, and therefore Lucia Costanza must have *seen* what was in the closet. Her husband, that poor fucking sod, had been killed by mistake. Jesus Christ!

Viciously Henchard jerked the cord of the television out of the wall and told himself miserably that there were now two women who knew about his treasure—that goddamn American woman Mary Kelly and the goddamn female procurator of San Marco, Lucia Costanza.

Thank God, he had moved quickly. The treasure was here, not there. They might know that it existed, but they didn't know where, and they would never, never find it. In this anonymous apartment, one of a thousand in this part of town, it was perfectly safe.

✶

T here was so much to tell Homer. Mary labored up the stairs of the house on Salizada del Pignater, painfully realizing that she would have to explain everything. Not just some of it, all of it.

Mary and Homer had been married a long time, not always comfortably. But there had been so many times when Mary had felt a warm wifely tenderness, critical moments when Homer had been nothing less than magnificent. Oh, once in a while he could be infuriating and impulsive, and sometimes he drifted off into otherworldly states, like now. But there had also been amazing occasions when he had gathered his wits and called upon his crazy transcendental intuition and then, *bang,* things would begin to happen. He was like a violinist who hits all the wrong notes but drives forward, ever forward, miraculously keeping up, arriving at the final chord with a triumphant sweep of his bow.

When she walked into the apartment Mary found Homer grubbing around in the kitchen, looking for something to eat. She led him to a chair and kissed him, then seized a loaf of bread and began slicing it, waving the knife dangerously in the air as she talked, sawing the loaf into pulverized pieces. "Homer, tell me what you know about the fate of the Jews in Venice during World War II."

Homer looked dazed. "Nothing much, I'm afraid. Are you about to tell me it was bad?"

"It was horrible. I bought a book. Wait a minute." Mary put down her knife and plucked the book out of her bag. "Here it is, the story of Venetian Jews from 1938 to 1945." She dropped it in Homer's lap and went back to her loaf of bread. "The deportation of Venetian Jews began in September 1943." The loaf of bread under Mary's knife disintegrated. She found another loaf and sliced it savagely in half. "It went on through 1944. Men, women, and children, old people, sick people. More than two hundred people went to death camps. Only four or five came back."

"My God." Homer got up and took Mary's knife. "Here, let me."

He began cutting clumsy slices while Mary threw open the refrigerator door. She took out a plate of prosciutto, slapped it on the table, and went on talking. "A few people hid themselves away in dark corners for years, like Anne Frank's family in Amsterdam. And in some of the synagogues they were afraid the Nazis would steal their Torah scrolls and Passover plates, so they hid them from the Germans for the duration. And then when the war was over they brought them out of hiding."

She began making sandwiches, not looking at Homer. He watched her, listening soberly. "I saw one of the hiding places. It's just been discovered. I mean, I saw what was in it." She snatched up a tray and began to gabble, because the hard part of the story was coming.

"And the things were made of gold, Homer, they were all made of gold, and there was a painting too, and some other things. And, oh, Homer, I forgot, we've got to call Sam. You know that picture I took, the one with the church we haven't been able to identify? The picture that shows the woman who's missing, the woman he's so anxious to find? Well, it's not a church, it's a synagogue. I was in the Ghetto Vecchio today and I recognized it, because that's where it is. Lucia Costanza was right there in front of the synagogue when I took the picture. Not now of course. I mean, I took the picture weeks ago." Mary scrabbled at the telephone on the wall. "I've got to call Sam."

Homer came up behind her and removed her hand from the phone and put his arm around her shoulders and made her sit down. His face was grave. "Mary, stop. Now tell me. Just slow down and tell me exactly how you happened to see what you saw. Come on now, start at the beginning. I've known for a while that something isn't right. Go ahead, my dear, just tell me."

She sat down, her heart throbbing, and began.

Later on in the privacy of the sitting room, while Mary sat in the kitchen staring miserably at the plate of uneaten sandwiches, Homer wrote a few words on a piece of paper. It was like a letter to a stranger named Homer Kelly, from another stranger of the same name—

*It hurts, it hurts, it hurts.*

He mailed the letter by dropping it carefully on the hearth, lighting it with a match, and standing with lowered head to watch it burn.

⌗

# CHAPTER 40

*H*omer was dumb with grief. As he left the house on Salizada del Pignater he glanced up at the top-floor window and saw Mary's pale face looking down. He was too shattered to wave. He trudged on, nodding politely at the men who were smoking and talking in front of the bar. They were all wearing boots, and he remembered the warning about high water. He had no boots, but what the hell.

The street was still dry, but when he came out on the Riva, water was lapping over the edge of the pavement. All the gondolas were smartly covered with blue canvas. The gondoliers were nowhere in sight. Across the water, San Giorgio Maggiore was a dreamlike half-ghostly shape. In the air there was a thin drizzle of mist and he had no umbrella. Homer didn't give a shit for an umbrella.

The first of the high-water duckboards began in front of the Church of Santa Maria della Pietà. Homer crossed a bridge, stepped off on the wooden platform, and tramped in the direction of the Piazzetta, stepping off to ascend another bridge, stepping off on another platform. He was one of an endless line of people moving forward, keeping to the right, everyone trying not to interfere with those coming the other way. The boards were barely wide enough for two to pass in single file. Homer's big frame was a problem. He had to walk crabwise, dangerously close to the edge.

The misting weather, the rising water, the ragged shreds of cloud hanging low overhead, everything matched the heaviness of his heart. But when he slopped into the Marciana his misery

FRANCESCO PETRARCA

MUSICA

21

was distracted by the organized confusion. Someone was shouting directions. Volumes from the rare book room were being carried up the stairs to the safety of the *primo piano*. Kids from the university who had come to the library to study and take notes had been drafted to pile chairs on tables and heave heavy books from the bottom shelves.

Some of Homer's normal response to an emergency came back when the official dragon shot out of her glass cage and shouted at him to help, *"Professore! Aiuto!"*

*"Sì, sì,"* I'll be right back," promised Homer. *"Ritorno immedi-atamente."* As he started up the stairs, someone thrust a pile of encyclopedias into his arms. Glancing back into the reading room he was amused to see the stone figure of Petrarch clutching his own book to his breast.

The office belonging to Dottor Samuele Bell, the curator of rare books, had become a control center. Signora Pino was on the phone, but she waved Homer into Sam's office. He pushed through a crowd of uniformed men from the Vigili Urbani who were awaiting orders. His friend Sam was almost invisible, sitting at his desk, bowed over a plan of the building.

He looked up and said, *"Un momento, Homer,"* and gave a final order. *"Non dimenticate! Le prese elettriche, dovete is-pezionarle, se vanno sottacqua."*

*"Sì, sì,"* said the sergeant in charge, and at once the crowd of young soldiers turned away and started down the stairs.

"What was that all about?" said Homer. *"Prese elettriche,* what's that?"

"Electric"—Sam flapped his hands—"holes? Connections? You know, Homer, this thing right here." He pointed at the baseboard behind his desk.

"Ah," said Homer, "you mean outlets, electrical outlets. Of course, I can see that water would mess up your entire electrical system."

Sam leaned back in his chair and rubbed his eyes. "We thought we were ready," he told Homer, "but we weren't. We have a plan with four teams, each with its own sector to take

care of, but in this emergency some people can't get here, so
we've had to scrubble up more manpower at the last minute. Is
that the right word? Scrubble? Scrobble?"

"Scrabble?" suggested Homer. "Sam, look." He reached
under his damp jacket, extracted the photograph of Lucia
Costanza from his breast pocket, and handed it to Sam. "The
building in the background isn't a church, it's a synagogue."

Sam took the picture and whooped. "A synagogue, of
course! That's why we couldn't find it by looking at pictures
of churches. My God, look at it! Those are Hebrew words over
the door. Which synagogue is it?"

"It's in the Ghetto Vecchio. Is there more than one
synagogue?"

"Of course, but it doesn't matter. Homer, the Ghetto Vecchio! That's where she is!"

"Well, maybe she is and maybe she isn't. It doesn't mean she
lives there."

"But it means we can look for her there. Homer, it's a place to
start."

Homer's heartsickness returned. His friend Sam was on the
verge of finding the woman he loved at the very moment Homer
was losing his. He turned abruptly away and drifted downstairs
to help with the fetching and carrying, while the water rose on
the Piazzetta and washed around the bases of the columns of
Saint Theodore and the lion of Saint Mark and reached the top
step of the long arcaded gallery of the Marciana.

Sam had done all he could. He slammed out of his office and
told Signora Pino that he was going out for an hour or two.

*"Ma, Dottore,"* objected Signora Pino, *"il suo programma!"*
She held up her copy of Sam's schedule. There were appointments with the chief of the polizia and a brigadiere capo from
the carabinieri.

*"Gli annulli,"* said Sam gaily, tossing his hand in the air. "Cancel them. Tell them the truth. Say I am ill."

"Ill? But, Dottore! You surely won't forget the appointment
at three o'clock!"

"Oh, that." Sam ran out of Signora Pino's office while she called after him, "Dottor Bell!" and flapped her appointment book.

He hadn't felt so nimble for ages. Like a boy skipping school Sam galloped down the stairs.

# CHAPTER 41

✖

*T*he Ospedale Civile did not look like a hospital. The famous facade on the square was not at all like the entrance to a place for the practice of modern medicine.

It had once been the headquarters of the Scuola Grande di San Marco, one of the ancient charitable confraternities of the city of Venice. Every pious and ambitious male citizen had belonged to one confraternity or another, helping to make its rules and choose its charities and lavish splendor on its great halls. But in 1797 that Antichrist Napoleon had wiped out all that was venerable and holy in the city, and since then there were no longer any processions of the dignified members of the Scuola Grande di San Marco. There were no public spectacles of Scuola members in monkish robes flagellating themselves, no *guardian grande* in a crimson toga marching across the bridge over the Rio dei Mendicanti in the company of his fellow *cittadini* and *nobili* in their robes of red and black.

Now instead of the music of the choristers of the old *scuola* there was only the murmur of tourists in the square, the soft flapping of pigeon wings, and the sirens of the *ambulanze* whizzing along the canal with flashing blue lights.

Out of sight behind the splendid old facade the hospital complex spread east and north in the direction of the lagoon. The modern offices and operating rooms and patient wards were scattered around five ancient cloisters. On the side facing the rio there were separate entries for the staff and an emergency entrance where patients could be hurried into

*Scuola di San Marco, Ospedale Civile*

the hospital. Some walked in on their own feet, some were carried on stretchers, some sat upright in rolling chairs like wheelbarrows.

The hospital was Doctor Richard Henchard's place of work. This afternoon he had come in great haste, half an hour late for his three o'clock appointment, addled by the confusion of settling Giovanna into the apartment on the Rio della Sensa. He would have neglected the appointment altogether if the man with the pancreatic carcinoma did not happen to be his most distinguished patient.

In spite of the rising water and the rain, Henchard was perspiring as he hurried past examining rooms and nurses' stations and toilets and crowded waiting rooms and the double doors of the chamber where he and his colleagues plied their sharp-edged trade. His nerves were at the breaking point. He had taken frantic action to protect his treasure, but the two women who knew it existed were still out there somewhere.

In his haste he was brought up short by his own office nurse, who looked at him with astonishment. "Oh, Doctor, there you are. We've been looking for you everywhere. Didn't you hear the intercom? Your patient is waiting. We have his X rays, and the CAT scans and ultrasound have just come in."

Henchard whirled into his office and charged into the examining room.

*"Buonasera,"* he said gruffly, snatching the envelope of X rays from the nurse.

His patient nodded politely, showing no sign of irritation after his long wait.

The man was a sad case. With his tumor it was surprising how long he had managed to stay ambulatory, but it couldn't last much longer. He had been given the option of enduring the hopeless eviscerating surgery of the Whipple procedure, but he had wisely declined.

Henchard withdrew an X ray from its envelope and smacked it up on the light screen. Under the quiet gaze of his patient, he looked at it for a while, then slapped up the ultrasound films and the CAT scan.

Swiftly he ran his eye over the eleven CAT cross sections and the ultrasound streaks and blobs, and then said curtly, "Take off your shirt and lie down."

Sam obliged. It didn't matter what the doctor was about to say. The news would be worse than last time, he knew that, but he smiled at Doctor Henchard as he laid aside his shirt, which slipped off the examining table and fell to the floor.

The doctor put his hands on the place where the mass had once been so evident, and grunted with satisfaction. He put his stethoscope on Sam's chest and listened. Then he stood back and said, "Put on your shirt."

Sam reached down to pick it up, and prepared himself for a final sentence of death. But Doctor Henchard seemed reluctant to speak. Sam buttoned his shirt and looked up at him serenely, to show that it was all right, that he was ready for the truth.

"I can't believe it," said Doctor Henchard. "It's a case in a thousand. Your liver and spleen and pancreas are all normal, the rales have cleared from your lungs, your X ray shows no sign of pneumonia. Your tumor is gone."

Sam stared at him, and murmured, "This is no time for a joke."

"It's not a joke, it's true. Last time the mass seemed smaller, but I thought I was imagining things. I wasn't. The malignancy has disappeared. I would call it a miracle if it didn't happen once in a great while, a complete remission." Henchard reached down automatically and picked up something that had dropped out of the patient's shirt pocket, and glanced at it as he handed it over.

It was a photograph of a woman. He recognized her. He snatched it back, and exclaimed, "Who's this? What's this?"

Sam was poised between the doomed serenity of a moment ago and tumultuous relief. Dreamily he reached for the picture of Lucia and said, "It's a friend. It's all right. I'm going to her. I'm going there right now."

The nurse spread the amazing news. Soon throughout the corridors of the hospital there was an excited buzz of talk. Some praised the doctor, some praised God, some attributed the miracle to the intervention of a newly discovered holy relic.

"What holy relic?" said one of the receptionists, pouring herself a cup of coffee.

"Haven't you heard?" said Henchard's nurse, taking all the credit. "Don't you know about the Veil of the Virgin? It's in Santo Spirito, my own parish. I pray to the Virgin's Veil for all Dottor 'Enciard's worst cases."

Before long everyone in the hospital knew about the recovery of Dottor Samuele Bell from pancreatic cancer, and about the precious veil of the Mother of God.

# CHAPTER 4 2

✂

There was a noise in the street, children's voices singing, loud rhythmical banging. Ursula ran to the window and looked down.

The children were clumping along in boots, walking in procession from one corner of the square to the other. They were banging on pots and pans and singing, *"San Martino! San Martino!"*

"Oh," cried Ursula. "It's Saint Martin's Day!" She ran to the kitchen.

"Ursula," said Mrs. Wellesley, "what are you doing?"

*Crash, crash!* Ursula came out of the kitchen with a great smile on her face, clashing two pot lids together. She told her grandmother, "I'm going too!"

"Never! Ursula, I forbid you. You are not to do anything so foolish." Mrs. Wellesley snatched the pot lids out of Ursula's hands. "The cult of saints, it's so ridiculous. Encouraging children to believe in such things, it's criminal."

"Oh, please." Ursula's small face crumpled as she began to cry.

"Certainly not. And besides, it's high water everywhere, the worst in years. Of course you can't go." Mrs. Wellesley herded her granddaughter into her bedroom and thrust a doll into her hands. It wasn't the one Ursula loved, the Barbie doll in the pale blue dress, the dress she had made herself with the help of Mrs. Kelly. It was the exquisite doll Mrs. Wellesley had bought at great price in a shop in San Polo. "Where's your sewing box, Ursula dear? Why don't you make her a new dress?"

Dorothea Wellesley was trying hard, but as usual she failed. Ursula handed back the doll and said primly, "No, thank you."

"Well, I give up." Mrs. Wellesley rolled her eyes and lifted her hands in bewilderment. Then she walked firmly across the room to Ursula's wardrobe and threw open the doors. The child had a secret stored away somewhere, but of course it was not here among her coats and play clothes and school uniforms. The birthday dress hung among the others as a rebuke and a disgrace, but everything else was just as usual.

She walked out, only casting an inquisitive glance at the dresser and the cupboard. Ursula's childish secret was surely behind those locked cupboard doors. Sooner or later her grandmother would find the key.

Her granddaughter had worn her out. Mrs. Wellesley yawned. She usually took a nap at about this time, but Ursula's school had been canceled because of high water. The child couldn't be trusted to behave herself alone without a pair of sharp eyes keeping track of her every move.

But Dorothea's eyes kept closing. She was a little tipsy with the wine she had indulged in at lunch. "Listen to me, Ursula," she said sleepily, "I'm just going to close my eyes for a minute. You may watch TV if you want, but I'm going to lock the outer door. I don't want you running around outside while I'm asleep."

Ursula looked down at her shoes and said nothing. But she was as crafty as her grandmother in purloining household keys.

Later that afternoon another parade of children marched down the street, clashing their pots and singing *"San Martino! San Martino!"* At the end of the procession marched Ursula Bell, singing the nonsense song with the rest—

> *"San Martino xe anda in sofita,*
> *a trovar ea so novisa,*
> *so novisa no ghe gera*
> *San Martin col cueo par tera!"*

# CHAPTER 43

✂

"I t's still leaking," said the hydraulic engineer from the Dipartimento Civile. "Look at that."

The exhausted *idraulici* could see it perfectly well, the narrow streams of water gushing around the edges of the iron barrier below the bridge over the Rio dei Miracoli. The rain had made a soup of the mud at the bottom of the drained canal. The tide was rising and the goddamn moon was at the full. In a couple of hours *acqua alta* would be at its peak. One of the men mopped his muddy face with his sleeve and shook his head in disgust. "It's only a fucking drop or two."

"No, no, it's too much. It's got to be absolutely watertight. You'll have to attach more *barriere* at both ends."

"What we really need is a miracle," suggested one of the men, snickering. "How about that new Veil of the Virgin? Why don't we pray to that?"

The response was a weary shuffling back to the task of heaving up another set of rusty metal plates and ramming them down with heavy sledgehammer blows to make the corrugations lap tightly together.

The engineer shook his head as they stepped back. Wordlessly he pointed to a thin trickle still streaming at the other end of the barrier. One of the men gave the offending plate a sharp kick. The trickle stopped.

*"Ecco!"* said the engineer, and they all laughed.

✂

The bishop's map of the distribution of high water clearly showed that part of the *sestiere* of Cannaregio would be perfectly dry. But, descending into a gondola at the Rialto Bridge with their stout British umbrellas, the two couples soon ran into another sort of problem.

One of the gondoliers was a tenor with a certificate from a conservatory in Verona. He was very expensive. While his colleague propelled the pretty craft along the Rio Fontego and the Rio dei Miracoli, he produced for their delectation ecstasies of vibrato and operatic sobs. Suddenly he broke off in the middle of a trill, said, *"Mamma mia,"* and lifted his pole from the water.

"Whatever is the matter?" said Louise Alderney, wife of the member of Parliament.

*"Qué pasa?"* said the bishop, adroitly producing an appropriate phrase.

His wife looked at him with contempt. "That's not Italian, Arthur, it's Spanish." She looked up sweetly at the gondolier, *"Per favore, signore, andiamo!"*

The gondolier tried to clarify the situation with excited gestures. Then he made a powerful sucking noise with his lips.

They looked at him with blank faces. The bishop stood up boldly and said, "I'll handle this." With a daring leap he landed on terra firma and ran up the steps of the little bridge over the blocked canal.

Below him four men with muddy boots looked up in surprise, unused to being addressed by red-faced members of the British clergy. The bishop spoke with heavy irony. "I must confess," he began, "that your fabled city is not quite living up to our expectations. How, may I ask, is our gondola to proceed?"

The gondolier had followed the bishop. Standing behind him he raised his eyebrows to the roots of his hair and shrugged his shoulders hugely. There followed a rapid exchange with the four muddy men in the drained canal. Soon they were all roaring with laughter.

"Oh, jolly good," said Elizabeth Cluff-Luffter, as her husband climbed clumsily back into the gondola.

"Three cheers, my lord," said Tertius Alderney, grinning.

"Hosanna in the highest!" warbled his wife Louise, who was an accomplished mezzo-soprano.

# CHAPTER 44

✜

*H*e found her. Or rather they found each other.

Lucia's borrowed rooms in the Ghetto Nuovo looked out on the trees in the middle of the square, and on the great wellhead from which the women of the ghetto had once drawn water. Today she sat at the window with her embroidery in her lap, alternately pulling her needle through the fabric and watching the comings and goings below.

With her embroidery she felt like an old Venetian grandmother, but her watchfulness was an anxious vigil. Lucia had no television in her small quarters, but the kindly old woman who sold lettuces and strawberries in the local shop had seen her face that morning on the screen. *"Che bella faccia! L'ho vista alla TV."*

Therefore the old woman was aware that the name Lucia was known by in the neighborhood was false, but she was a tender-hearted old lady and she said she would not give Lucia away.

*"Lei, non è ebrea?"* asked Lucia.

*"No, sono cattolica,"* said the old woman, and she promised to pray for Lucia.

Well, it was terrible news. If she had been seen on television there might be other local people who would call the polizia. Lucia sat at the window and kept her eyes open for the approach of official-looking persons or men in uniform. Her bag was packed. She was ready to bolt by a back door.

But she was not afraid of the children. On the day of extreme high water she saw them wading barefoot in the square. They were floating paper boats called *Regina* and *Maria* and *Guido* and *Franco*. Quickly Lucia made one of her own from a piece of scrap paper, then pulled off her shoes and ran down to join them.

"From this tree," commanded Maria, "to that tree." Carefully they lined up their fragile craft. Lucia set hers down in the shallow water with the others. "Go!" cried Maria, and with excited screams the children released their boats and watched them rock gently forward. "Not fair!" screeched Maria, as Guido puffed out his cheeks and blew his boat ahead of the rest.

Now they were all puffing and blowing. Lucia laughed, but she stopped laughing when she caught a glimpse of a tall stranger crossing the bridge. At once she ran splashing back to the safe haven of her own doorway and hurried upstairs.

Sam had been wandering around the Ghetto Vecchio and the Ghetto Nuovo for half an hour, afraid to ask anyone the whereabouts of Lucia Costanza. After all, she was the object of a search by the police. By the time he saw the children he had almost given up. Disconsolate, he smiled at them, and he smiled at their paper boats, which were folded yellow sheets from the Pagine Gialle, or pink pages from *La Gazzetta dello Sport*. He smiled at the names scrawled on them—*Regina*, *Franco*, *Guido*, *Maria*, *Lucia*.

He picked up the boat called *Lucia*. It was not yellow or pink. It was a folded piece of white paper on which he could make out part of a letterhead—*di San Marco.*

*"Dov' è Lucia?"* he asked quickly.

One of the girls shook her head and laughed. *"No, no. Non è Lucia! La donna si chiama Sofia."*

*"Ma allora, è una donna, non una ragazza?"*

*"Sì, sì, è la Signora Sofia."*

*"Va bene. Dov' è la Signora Sofia?"*

At once they all pointed, and Sam looked up to see a woman standing at an upstairs window, looking down at him. With her dark hair flowing over her shoulders she looked younger than he remembered, but there was no mistaking the face that had so captivated him on the day he had walked into her office. Rapturously, cautiously, he called to her, *"Signora Sofia?"*

Impulsively, without thinking, Lucia leaned out the window and called, *"Dottor Bell?"*

For a moment they gazed at each other as though stunned, and then Lucia turned away, ran down the stairs, and opened the door.

He was running toward her, splashing in his rubber boots. It had begun to rain. The children hurried away. As he stopped in front of her there was no one else in the square.

She could think of nothing to say. Nor could he. At last he said huskily, "Are you all right, Dottoressa?"

"Oh, yes. Are you?"

"Yes, I am," he said eagerly, saying it truthfully for the first time. "Yes, yes, I'm very much all right."

Lucia couldn't help laughing. There was something so amusing about his face and voice. She remembered that he had made her laugh before. Now he said something else, but so softly that she missed it. "What did you say?"

"I said, what if someone were to hold your hand?"

Oh, how deliciously ridiculous! It was a continuation of the absurd moment in her office that day in October, the scene she had been playing and replaying so often in her head.

She smiled and looked away from him at the wet iron lid of the wellhead and the dark wet trunks of the trees. "Well, of course, it would depend on who it was."

"Me. It would be me."

A wave of hilarity swept over Lucia, and she began to laugh again.

He laughed too, and said, "Well? What do you think?"

"I don't know. Perhaps we could try it just as an experiment."

At once he grasped her hand and lifted it to his lips, and murmured, "Is the experiment working?"

Lucia couldn't stop laughing. "It's too soon to tell. Experiments usually take longer."

They waded across the square together in the misty rain,

her hand clasped in his, and crossed the bridge into the Ghetto Vecchio.

Then he stopped walking and turned to her with another insane question. "What if I were to kiss you? I mean, right here in front of this good rabbi?"

The rabbi raised his black hat and smiled.

"You mean"—Lucia could hardly speak—"another experiment?"

"Yes, yes, just an experiment."

She closed her eyes as his face came near. Gently, without holding her, he kissed her lips lightly, then withdrew and murmured, "Did it work?"

"Oh, oh, I'm not quite sure." Lucia kept her eyes closed, and he tried again, putting his hands on her shoulders, kissing her seriously.

It was so lovely, so enchanting. Lucia stood perfectly still like a flower in the field, as he wrapped his arms around her and said softly, "I wasn't sure I still knew how to kiss a girl."

"It's like riding a bicycle," she whispered. "It's something you don't forget."

"Oh, God, Lucia, Lucia."

It was beginning to rain in earnest. She took his hand and led him back over the bridge to her house. The door was unlocked. Lucia drew Sam inside and led the way upstairs, leaving the door open behind her. The rising water opened it farther still. It swayed on its hinges.

Neither of these mature, highly educated and distinguished people cared that they had previously known each other for less than half an hour.

❂

Richard Henchard stood outside, shielding himself from the rain under a tree. His astonishing patient, so miraculously recovered, had led him straight to Lucia Costanza.

What was the goddamn woman doing now? Well, naturally, she was about to go to bed with a famous scholar, Henchard's prize example of a pancreatic carcinoma remission, Signor Samuele Bell, who now had a lifetime of delightful fuckings ahead of him. Goddamn his vanished cancer! Goddamn his healthy balls! And goddamn his perfect ears, which might now be listening eagerly to any goddamn thing the woman might feel like telling him, between fucking endearments and fucking embraces and goddamn fucking orgasms! Henchard groaned aloud. *Oh, God, he had no time, he had no time!*

Then time opened out before him. The rain came down harder than ever, but someone rushed out of Signora Costanza's door and hurried away under an umbrella. It was his patient, Samuele Bell.

Had there been a lover's quarrel already? Henchard grinned and reached in his pocket. His weapon was warm in his hand, but he kept it out of sight as he started for the door. Now, thanks be to God, he would find her alone, and then he could do with her whatever he wanted.

✂

M ary had known it would be miserably uncomfortable,
but she had been unprepared for the extent of the
wreckage. She had hit Homer hard. Recalling the glib
bragging stories of her friends, she could not remember any tal-
lying up of the costs. Had they been as terrible as this?

She looked at her watch. It was three o'clock. She couldn't
go to bed and indulge in a fit of weeping. *There was no time.*
She had to go out again, she had to take a vaporetto to Cannaregio and find her way back to the Rio della Sensa. She had
to get back there before Richard took everything away. If she
could get hold of one thing from that closet, just one many-
branched candlestick or Passover plate, then she could take it to
somebody—the polizia?—the carabinieri?—and they would believe her when she said that something next door to Tintoretto's
house smelled to high heaven.

It would do no good to accuse someone called Visconti. She
had once tried to call Doctor Richard Visconti at the hospital,
but there had been nobody there by that name. In escorting her
around the city he had obviously been two-timing his wife. Mary
was no fool, she had figured it out, but she had managed not to
care.

Now she rummaged furiously in her dresser drawers, looking
for the picture of Visconti. When she found it, she tore it in little
pieces, but instead of throwing them in the wastebasket she
opened the pages of the book she had bought in the Ghetto
Nuovo and dropped them inside. Now the torn scraps of the
photograph of Doctor Richard Visconti were folded between

photographs of men and women who had been deported to
death camps—

SI RICERCA PAOLA SONINO
ARRESTATA IL 28 GENNAIO 1944.

CHI AVESSE NOTIZIE DI COLOMBO ANGELO
È PREGATO DI DARE LE NOTIZIE
ALLA COMUNITÀ ISRAELITICA.

Then she washed the tears off her cheeks, stuffed her red umbrella into the side pocket of her bag, and pulled on her boots,
because *acqua alta* had been bad enough this morning, and the
radio predicted *acqua altissima alle cinque.* The worst was coming at five o'clock, the highest water yet.

It took her an hour to get across the city. By four o'clock she
was wading in deep water past the figure of the Moor on the
corner and the second Moor beside Tintoretto's house, and
along the pavement inundated by the overflowing Rio della
Sensa, to the door she had entered that morning in such a dizzy
state of desire—could it really have been only this morning?

She touched the handle of the door, her heart beating. To her
surprise it opened easily, but before she could go inside, she was
hailed by a shout from above. She looked up. A woman stared
down at her from the window of the apartment.

*"Prego, signora, chi è lei?"*

The question was hostile, the face glowering.

*"Sono un' americana, mi chiamo Mary Kelly. Dov' è il Dottore?"*

It took her a little while to allay the suspicions of Giovanna,
but at last she was permitted to come upstairs. Giovanna spoke
no English, but Mary's blatant lie in Italian soon mollified her.
Thinking fast, Mary claimed to be the former tenant. On leaving
the apartment this morning she had packed up something belonging to the dottore. *"Ecco!"* Mary pulled her notebook out of
her bag. *"Questo appartiene al dottore. Qual' è il suo indirizzo?"*
What is his address?

Giovanna beckoned her to the window and put out her plump pink arm. The nail of her pointing finger was enameled in silver. *"Calle de la Madonna, vicino al Rio dei Gesuiti."* Looking down at the lake of water below the window, she made shooing motions with her hands. *"Maledetta quest' acqua alta!"*

But when Mary descended to ground level, the water was deeper than ever.

She had come too late. Visconti had already removed his golden horde. The closet where it had lain, glittering and mysterious, was wide open, but it was empty. The sleeping bag on which they had made love had also been taken away, replaced by puffy comforters and pillows belonging to his girlfriend.

The treasure was gone.

# CHAPTER 46

✖

*H**e could do with her whatever he wanted.*
There was only one thing Henchard wanted to do with Lucia Costanza. The gun that had killed her husband was heavy in his pocket. Lorenzo Costanza's death had been a mistake, but hers was a necessity. She was a rat gnawing at the edges of his treasure.

That had been the trouble from the beginning, proliferating vermin. Now, shit! There were two of them, a couple of female rats, and both of them had seen what they shouldn't have seen. Both of them knew about the gold plates and the gold scrolls and the gold candlesticks, both of them had seen the painting. Oh, Christ, the painting! The Titian, it had to be a Titian! A Titian worth a fabulous sum if he could figure out how to put it on the market.

No, there was only one thing to do with the bloody woman. He couldn't do it here. A couple of men were making a lot of noise on the ground floor, talking and arguing and shoving furniture around. If he did it here, Christ, they'd come barging up to find out what the hell was going on.

Henchard walked up the stairs into Lucia's apartment and took her away at gunpoint. She had no time to gather her wits, no time to write a message, no time to snatch up her umbrella or put on her boots. Poking the muzzle of the gun deep into the flesh of her back, he thrust her before him down the stairs and out into the rain. Then, through shallow and deep water, he gripped her by the arm and marched her across a mile of

Cannaregio to the very door of the flat from which he had so recently ousted Giovanna.

It was a long way. Lucia was a tall strong woman, and at first she squirmed and tried to pull herself free, but he only hissed in her ear and held her tighter. Because of the rain and rising water there was no one on the Campo di Ghetto Nuovo, or on the bridge leading out of the ghetto to the north, or on the Fondamenta della Misericordia, or on the narrow zigzagging ways beyond the end of the Rio de la Misericordia—no one to whom she could call for help, only a few dogged umbrellas held low over crouching unseen heads. On the bridge over the Rio di Felice she cried out to an elderly woman who was dragging a cart up the steps, and the old woman, startled, looked up at her and said, *"Signora?"*

But at once Lucia was wrapped in a violent embrace and a hard mouth was crushed against hers, and the muzzle of the gun was jammed painfully into her side—it was the very same *modello molto popolare* with which Richard Henchard had murdered her husband, but Lucia did not know that.

From then on she walked mechanically with streams of water running down her face and her clammy skirt sticking to her legs. She was tormented by the conviction that nothing mattered anyway, not anymore, because it was painfully obvious what had really happened. It had been Sam Bell himself who had betrayed her. He had not looked for her because he loved her, he had looked for her because for some insane reason he wanted to hand her over to this highly presentable thug. The logic was inescapable. *Why had the thug appeared so soon after Sam had left her alone, pretending to be going out for wine?*

⠯

When Sam ran back to Lucia's house with the bottle of wine, his rubber boots sloshed easily through the overflow from the surrounding canals. The door of the house was still ajar, nudged open by the push of the water.

Behind the apartment door on the ground floor male voices were talking loudly, and there was a clatter and bump of furniture. He had to step aside as a couple of men came out with a sofa, grunting and sweating. He smiled at them and ran joyfully up the stairs. Lucia's door was wide open. Walking in, he called, "Lucia!"

There was no answer. He called her again, "Lucia, where are you?"

Again there was only silence. For the next five minutes Sam walked from room to room, not believing she could be gone. But no Lucia emerged from the bathroom, fresh from the shower. No Lucia waited for him in the bedroom, holding out her arms.

She was not in the apartment at all. Lucia was gone.

He galloped downstairs and knocked loudly on the door of the ground-floor flat.

Again there was only a vacant silence. Staring out into the square, he looked for the two men with the sofa, but they had vanished.

There was only one wretched conclusion. Sam closed his eyes and leaned against the jamb of the door, perfectly understanding what had happened. He had been too outrageous. Lucia had come to her senses and run away.

The rain had turned to mist, then rain again. Sam pulled the collar of his jacket up around his ears and started across the rising lake of water in the square, telling himself that his new lease on life was no good to him if there was nothing left to live for. Yesterday nothing had mattered. Today everything did. He could no longer be careless because he was no longer dying.

☒

"Upstairs," Henchard told Lucia. "Go ahead. Get upstairs."

Unwillingly Lucia climbed. She wanted to turn around and shove him down the stairs, but she was afraid. What in hell did this man want with her? And who in God's name was he? After

a desperate half hour in his company she knew she had seen him
fleetingly before, but when and where?

At the top of the stairs Henchard reached around her and unlocked the door of the apartment. "Go ahead," he said, "go in."

Lucia walked slowly into the room, avoiding a heap of plastic-
wrapped objects in one corner. A gilt chair lay on its side. A bed
had been stripped of its sheets. Beside the bed a wardrobe door
hung open, displaying a tangle of empty hangers. The floor was
littered with miscellaneous household trash, a pink wastebasket,
a dirty lavender towel, a pair of pink panty hose, a broken hand
mirror, a blow-dryer, a long strip of lavender toilet paper, a scattered deck of cards. Was this dreary room the last place she was
ever to see?

"Stand over there against the wall."

"I will not." Cornered and terrified, Lucia lunged at Henchard. He staggered backward, regained his balance and fired,
and at once she fell to the floor in an awkward crumpled heap,
blood pooling under her body, soaking the scattered panty hose
and staining bright red the jack of spades.

Henchard stood over her, breathing hard. *One rat down, one
rat to go.*

God, that was the trouble. There was always one more. You
chased a couple of vermin into a room and they scrambled
around and darted into corners and disappeared under furniture, and when you trapped one of them, the other darted out
the door. The goddamn lady professor from America, Mary
Kelly, where in hell was she now? She was the second rat, and
the room in which she was running free was the entire city of
Venice. He had to find her. *Now, right now! Because there was
no time.*

Henchard stepped over Lucia as if she were a dead dog and
went into the bathroom to relieve the pressure on his bladder.
Afterward he looked in the mirror, slicked back his hair, and left
the flat, locking the door behind him with extreme care.

And then the missing rat ran straight into his hands. When

Henchard flung open the street door, Mary Kelly was walking straight toward him along the narrow street, carrying a red umbrella.

❈.

Listening upstairs, Lucia heard a shot ping against a wall. She sat up, feeling quite well. Her arm was bleeding, but the blood was only seeping out. She felt fine, amazingly fine, in fact nothing hurt at all.

Just as a precaution she reached for the pair of panty hose and tied it above the place where the cartridge had creased her arm, using her teeth to tighten the pink nylon just enough to stop the seepage. Then she stood up shakily and looked at the heap of clumsy packages in the corner. They seemed to have no relation to the litter of household refuse on the floor. Lucia walked slowly across the room and got down on her knees. Feebly she tugged at the plastic knot of one of the bags and took out a thick object wrapped in yellowed newsprint and tied with string.

The name of the newspaper was clearly visible under a layer of dust—

### GAZZETTA DI VENEZIA
#### DOMENICA 5 DICEMBRE 1943

# CHAPTER 47

☒

M ary ran.

Henchard ran faster.

She ran into Campo Madonna, but he was right behind her.

The skin of Mary's back shuddered as she slopped into
the square, but there were two or three people in Campo
Madonna—surely it was not a place where a man with a gun
would be so stupid as to fire a shot. Glancing over her shoulder,
she saw him pause and slip around the corner.

For the moment he was gone, but of course he wasn't
really gone, because he must be planning to seize her when she
moved out of Campo Madonna into the *calle* heading south,
zigzagging out of Cannaregio in the direction of San Marco, because of course she *had* to go south, and the man she knew as
Richard Visconti must surely know that she had to go south.

So it was something like a miracle, the tall woman coming out
of the little shop on the other side of the square, carrying a plastic sack heavy with oranges in one hand and holding a newspaper over her head with the other. Mary nearly ran into her,
and for a moment, startled, they looked straight into each
other's eyes. Then without a word Mary thrust the red umbrella
at her and ran past her into the shop.

The rain was falling heavily now. Henchard was sick of it. He
was sick of struggling through drizzle and cloudburst and high
water to free himself from one dangerous woman after another.
He was weary of being soaked to the skin, fed up with the watery

cataracts that sheeted down his forehead and stuck his lashes together until he was nearly blind.

But not blind enough to miss the red umbrella. When it passed him, moving south in the right direction, he hurried after it.

Only when it stopped to hail another umbrella, only when the two umbrellas came together amid a storm of jolly Venetian gossip, the two women talking loudly both at once, standing in water up to the ankles of their boots, did Henchard discover his mistake.

But by this time Mary Kelly had found a way around him. For the moment she was in the clear. The rain had stopped. People in rubber boots were emerging into the narrow streets. Mary set a course for Saint Mark Square, heading south, ever south. She was lost only once, when she chose a dead end. Retracing her steps, she discovered a bridge across Rio di San Marina and plunged on in the right direction.

But when she found herself once more in familiar territory, she was obviously too far to the east. Correcting her mistake, she hurried across the dry pavement of Campo San Zaccaria, heading for the Riva and the lagoon.

But then she stopped short, her heart in her mouth. Henchard was there. He had found her again.

꘍

*"San Martino! San Martino!"* Crash! Crash! Crash! Ursula marched at the end of the parade of children, clashing her pot lids and singing, *"San Martino! San Martino!"* Her father was dying! She had heard it on the telephone! She would not let him die! *"San Martino! San Martino!"*

Sister Maddalena led the procession along a route where the streets were dry. When they met another parade of children Ursula abandoned Sister Maddalena's because it was turning back. She didn't want to go back. There was nothing for her at home but another scolding. The new parade was marching away from home, they were going the other way. Their pots and pans were noisier, *CRASH! CRASH!* Their singing was even louder, *"SAN MARTINO! SAN MARTINO!"*

When she saw Mrs. Kelly hurrying toward her, Ursula also saw the man running behind her, and instantly she knew what to do. She stopped short. The girls behind her cannoned into her back, but she had made an opening, and Mrs. Kelly ran straight through it, gasping, *"Grazie, Ursula."*

And then there was a scene of chaos. Ursula crowded forward, and the gap in the procession became a knot. Henchard slammed right into it, and now all of them were rolling on the damp pavement, four screaming little girls in blue uniforms and a cursing man in a three-piece suit.

Had she lost him? Mary had been heading for the Riva, but now she turned back. There was only one other way to go, but it was the right way. Mary had a compass inside her head, and she knew she was heading west. She couldn't be very far from Piazza San Marco and the Piazzetta and the Biblioteca Marciana. And there in the Marciana she would find Homer, and it was Homer she so desperately wanted.

She ran quickly, dodging around a man with a cell phone against his ear, then encountering a stoppage at a jovial meeting of two old friends.

*"Ciao! Come stai, tutto bene?"*

*"Sì, grazie, e tu?"*

*"Bene, bene, grazie!"*

*"Ciao! Ci vediamo!"*

*"Ciao! A presto!"*

They parted and at last Mary ran past them to an intersection, a little square with a church, where her progress was again obstructed. Even in her haste and confusion she recognized the two young people blocking her way. They were still in costume, still calling out *"Concerti!"* and holding their tickets high. The boy was still scrappily dressed in a grubby brocaded coat, but his bare feet were inches deep in water. The girl still wore her panniered skirt, but the hem was below the waterline. They looked at her curiously and called out, *"Concerto, signora?"*

*"No, no, grazie!"* Mary shook her head and dodged through a *sottoportico,* hoping to find a detour on the other side. But it was only a courtyard, a dead end, a mistake. She couldn't stay here. Catching her breath, she hid behind a scaffolding bearing a sign, COMUNE DI VENEZIA LAVORI, and peered around it to look back.

At once she saw Henchard run up to the ticket-selling kids and stop. He was gesturing excitedly, asking a question. To her horror she saw the boy in the brocaded coat and the girl in the wide skirt responding, flinging out their arms—but they were pointing the wrong way!

Back again in the little square, Mary gave the ticket sellers a glowing look, and galloped away in the direction of Piazza San Marco. At once she ran into deeper water.

There was nothing to do but splash straight into it. Her boots were too short. The water poured over their tops and engulfed her feet. It was like walking in filled buckets. Her trousers were soaked to the knees.

Most of the people on the street had taken heed of the warning siren. They were moving confidently through the running stream with their feet dry inside their tall boots. One boy carried his girlfriend on his back. A fashionably dressed woman minced along in stocking feet, holding up her skirt with one hand and her shoes with the other. A family of Korean tourists had been supplied by their hotel with plastic trash bags, and they shuffled through the water doggedly, holding the bags around their hips, heading slowly in the direction of San Marco and the expensive shops on the Mercerie. They looked glum. Galumphing past them, Mary guessed they were feeling cheated—*was it for this they had paid so many millions of won to take a once-in-a-lifetime tour?* Their gloom increased as the rain began again.

Mary missed her umbrella. She was thankful to climb out of deep water onto the steps of a bridge. On the other side she was of course in deep water again, but now she could see the domes of San Marco. Looking back, she saw no sign of her pursuer, and she sloshed confidently through the Piazzetta dei Leoni into the piazza, which had become a lake.

But here at last the duckboards began, and like everyone else she could step up on the wooden platform and hurry along in single file toward the square, while another parade of people streamed past her the other way, cocking their umbrellas sideways.

But it was no good. Just as the huddled procession in front of her passed the first of the five entrances to the basilica, Mary glanced back and saw between the umbrellas the piercing dark eyes of Richard Visconti, the man who had followed her so far across the city, over a score of little bridges and through a labyrinth of narrow streets and little squares bearing the names of saints. Now he was moving rapidly forward on the same platform of narrow planks, staring around someone's shoulder. She could hear him shout, *"Andiamo, signore,"* because the timid old man in front of him had stopped in his tracks, jostled by umbrellas, frightened by the advancing column rushing past him, afraid of tipping off into the water.

In the clock tower high above the piazza the two half-naked bronze giants swung their hammers against the bell. Solemnly it bonged five times, dropping its echoing vibrations over the square, shivering the green water. Below them the gold leaf on the winged lion of Saint Mark sparkled in the rain, as he held open with one paw his famous book to show the blessing of the angel of God, the words that were the pride of Venice, its glory and triumph. Under him another symbol of the city sat enthroned, the Virgin Mary with her child.

No one looked up at these monumental reminders of the greatness of Venice. Everyone in the square was engrossed by the watery problem at hand.

The problem was nothing new to Richard Henchard. He was perfectly accustomed to high water. Unfortunately he had left his boots at home under the coatrack by the door—where his wife discovered them later on, so she called the hospital to urge him to come for them, but his nurse said, *"Mi dispiace, Signora 'Enciard,* the doctor was here for an appointment, but then he went out again. Have you heard about the miracle?" and when

Vittoria said warily, "No, what miracle?" the nurse told her the whole story about the recovery of one of her husband's patients with the help of the Virgin's Veil.

There was only one miracle that Henchard needed now, and that was a guarantee of the safety of his billions of lire, those billions upon billions for which he had already taken so much trouble. With extraordinary care he had identified the dangers, he had removed them one by one, silencing forever those other interfering claims. Now there was only a single claimant left, the woman hurrying ahead of him across the square, the last of the rats, darting here, darting there, trying to escape, but she would never escape. He was close now, very close. If only the old idiot in front of him would move a little faster! *"Vada avanti, signore!"*

But the old man was frightened. His cane slipped on the wet boards. He slowed down and stopped. Henchard cursed and jumped off into the water. It was above his knees, but he surged forward, passing half a dozen other creeping fools.

It was a tactical mistake. Mary jumped off on the other side. Now there was a moving human wall between them. She lunged forward, dragging her heavy legs, sending up foaming splashes left and right, catching glimpses of Visconti in flashes between hurrying raincoats and dangling cameras.

Beside them loomed the basilica in all the frolicsome giddiness of its clustered columns and mosaics, its golden lion and winged angels and gesturing saints and delicate pointed cupolas. And above the columns and angels and saints and cupolas rose the strange wild domes like a vision out of the *Arabian Nights*. Another set of platforms had been provided as an approach to the central portal, and at the junction with the north–south stream of traffic there was a teetering confusion of tourists and tossing umbrellas.

Once again Henchard was blocked. Looking back, Mary saw him leap up into the middle of the tangle and force his way across. When she dared to look again, nothing lay between them but a broad sheet of water, pockmarked with rain. Running for her life, heaving her slow legs through a tide of water two feet high, Mary had a heartsick vision of home—of a dreamy autumn day on Fairhaven Bay, her paddle dipping silently in the dark river and a great blue heron motionless on the shore. Shuddering, she felt again the wincing place in the small of her back as though her drenched denim jacket were painted like a marksman's target. She was exhausted, her heart was throbbing, but she had to keep trying, she had to reach the long arcade that stretched away beyond the campanile.

There she would surely be safe, swallowed up in the seething mass of people trying to escape the deep water in the square. Mary plowed on, dragging her feet in their heavy rubber buckets. On the south side of the square the little plastic chairs and tiny tables belonging to Florian's were piled in disappointed heaps, but the jazz piano was plunking out a show tune. Florian's was doing its best to whip up a little cheer in spite of the rain and high water.

Closer, she was closer now, she was almost there, she was very near. But not near enough, because she could hear Visconti splashing closer and closer behind her, he was catching up with her, he had her by the arm!

She whirled to face him, and at once he gripped her by both arms. "No, no," sobbed Mary, trying to wrench herself free. She pulled away, then lost her balance and fell on hands and knees. She was breast-deep in seawater. Henchard laid rough hands on her shoulders and tried to jerk her upright, but then other hands were helping her, lifting her gently.

"*Sta bene, signora?*"

"*Oh, signora, ha bisogno di qualcosa?*"

Two women were holding her, mopping at the drenched front of her jacket, helping her along. Henchard slopped after them, nearly bumping against Mary's back as the women supported her up the shallow steps. What was she telling them? Oh, God, there was no time, there was no time.

It was the thickest crowd Mary had ever seen. The thousands

of tourists who normally spread themselves over the broad
square, ambling in all directions, buying postcards, feeding pigeons, and taking pictures of each other, were now condensed
and squeezed together under the arcades that stretched around
the piazza and the Piazzetta. Even here the cresting tide washed
high around their legs, but they were talking and laughing
loudly, seeming to take pleasure in the extremity of the crisis.

For Mary the close pressure was just what she wanted, and
she was sorry when the two women withdrew their arms and
said courteously, *"Sta bene?"* and slipped away.

Visconti was still there. He was right behind her, treading on
her heels, pushing up against her back. She turned and hissed at
him, "Piss off!" but he only stared at her blankly as she tried to
edge between thickets of elderly people who were trailing the
lifted banner of their tour guide.

The entrance to the Marciana was very near. Mary could see
the welcoming figures of the two tall statues in the doorway,
their bare toes underwater. Then Visconti grabbed her from the
back and his gun rammed against her spine. She couldn't free
herself, she could only drag him after her through the door into
the pool of water in the vestibule and up beyond the coatroom
and past the dragon's lair. The glass cage was empty, but the
place was milling with people.

They looked at her in surprise, their mouths open, and at last
Henchard came to his senses and tried to back away. But suddenly Homer was there, gaping at them through the glass door
of the rare book room. Mary stretched out her arms and called
his name.

Homer was no athlete, everybody knew that, but he was six
feet six inches tall and a lot broader and heavier than Richard
Henchard. He dropped the books he was carrying on the wet
floor—Marin Sanudo's *De origine, situ et magistratibus urbis
venetae* and Martino da Canal's *Les estoires de Venise*—and,
barging through the glass door, he knocked Henchard down.

CHAPTER 48

✄

A nd then Henchard got away.

In the wild scramble of clutching hands, bewildered scholars and horrified librarians, in the clumsy flailing of the students who had been moving books from low shelves to high shelves in the reading room, with Mary shouting at the top of her lungs and Homer punching out in all directions, the man at the center of the commotion melted away.

"Where is he?" cried Mary, staring furiously around.

"My God," said Homer. He bounded down the hall toward the outer door, slithering sideways in the water below the coatroom, nearly losing his balance. Bursting out into the arcade he collided with a flood of men and women from Denmark who were taking refuge from the rain. More participants in the holiday tour from Copenhagen poured up from the motor launch that had transported them from their hotel.

Homer squeezed through the soggy crowd of Danes and craned his neck to stare down the length of the Molo. Mary caught up with him and caught his arm and looked too. They could not see Henchard, but they could see a moving wave of staggering Scandinavians and hear them shouting, *"Hold op! Hold op!"*

Mary pointed and shrieked, "There he goes."

Again they were too late. By the time they had shoved their way to the vaporetto stop, butting through another procession of indignant tourists from Copenhagen, Henchard's hired water taxi was veering away from the slip, heading out into the lagoon.

Within five minutes half a dozen powerboats of the special

force of the carabinieri, the Nucleo Natanti, were after him, but the directions they had been given were conflicting. A hundred hands pointed left, right, and straight across the water, and a dozen voices on emergency line 112 shouted, *Lido, Giudecca, the Giardini.*

Mary Kelly's was the only voice of reason. With Homer's arm wrapped tightly around her she stood dripping in the carabinieri station in Campo San Zaccaria and drew her finger across a map. "Try here," she said thoughtfully. "Try the Rio dei Gesuiti."

Her hair hung in sopping strings across her face and her clothes were waterlogged, but her voice was authoritative, and they took her advice.

# C H A P T E R 4 9

✄

*L*ucia heard the thumping approach on the stairs. At once she got to her feet and hobbled into the bathroom. Her arm had begun to throb painfully.

The latch looked feeble. It had lost a screw. Lucia shot the bolt across, then leaned her back against the door to brace it. She was sickeningly aware that she could not be allowed to co-exist in the same world with the precious things in the next room, the Torah scrolls, the seven-branched candlesticks, the Passover plates, the Raphael, the illuminated manuscripts from the library of Cardinal Bessarion, and the most celebrated single work from the Aldine press, *The Dream of Poliphilius*. A choice between all of those things on the one hand and this miscella-neous and irrelevant woman on the other was no choice at all. They would stay, she would go.

The clumping footsteps stopped. A key rattled in the lock.

*Coraggio, Lucia.* She put her ear against the bathroom door and listened, her eyes filling with tears. Her ridiculous momen-tary happiness was about to come to an end. It had been too good to be true.

But for Richard Henchard, Lucia Costanza's life or death was of no interest any longer. He failed even to notice that she was no longer lying on the floor. He had lost interest in everything reasonable and sane, he had forgotten every sensible concern with cause and effect. His mind was empty of everything but the passion of possession—*these things are mine.*

He was not the first man to lose his sanity to a dream of fabu-lous riches, a vision of gold coins glistening in wobbling patterns under the sea, the sound of a shovel thunking against the buried lid of a strongbox. The difference between Henchard and all the other madmen pursuing fantastic dreams of unimaginable wealth was that his own treasure had been *found,* he *possessed* it, it was right here under his hand.

Lucia could hear him cursing. He had left his trophies securely wrapped, and now they had been taken out of their wrappings and exposed. It was another mark against his prisoner. Once again she braced her whole weight against the door.

But nothing happened. There was no howl of accusation, no violent smashing of the cracked panels of the bathroom door. There was only the sound of heavy breathing, the scraping of objects across the floor, a loud clanging as something was dropped, and for a moment a discordant jangling of the bells on the Torah scrolls. She could hear his grunts and curses, and again and again the thump of his feet on the stairs, going rapidly down and slowly up, down and up, and finally down for good.

Was he gone? Lucia held her breath. She waited for ten minutes before softly unlocking the bathroom door and looking out. She was alone. Quietly she walked into the next room and gazed at the floor where the treasure had lain.

It was gone, it was all gone but for a few yellowed pieces of paper blowing across the floor. Turning, she saw that the breeze came from the staircase. The door of her prison stood wide open.

# CHAPTER 50

✄

*L*ike a mother tucking a baby into a perambulator, adjusting the pillow and arranging the blankets just so, Henchard bowed over the objects in the cart and shifted them this way and that.

First he tried putting the painting on the bottom. Then he leaned it upright against the side. The gold plates went in flat, with the book resting on top of them. The Torah scrolls were too long for the cart, so he had to set them in at an angle, and then the tarpaulin kept slipping off the jeweled crowns on the ends of the long handles. The bells jingled and jangled.

It had stopped raining. The tide was going down. The high water that had drenched his trousers during his frantic pursuit of the goddamn American woman was now only a few puddles here and there, but the legs of his pants were still wet. They stuck unpleasantly to Henchard's shins as he began racing the cart along Calle de la Madonna. Luckily it was getting dark. *Right turn coming up, left on Calle Varisco, then straight across Campiello Stella.*

So far, so good. It was all backstreets, not broad avenues like the Strada Nuova. But the hospital was not yet in sight, and there would soon be busy places like Campiello Widman to get across.

As a hiding place for his jingling Torah scrolls and his golden plates and his beautiful old manuscripts and his precious Titian painting, the hospital was a desperate temporary fallback, but if he could get the cart across Rio de la Panada and Rio dei Mendicanti and take it in by the tradesmen's entrance to a certain very capacious closet, then everything would be okay—Henchard remembered the closet particularly because he had once been cornered inside it by an aggressive little nurse's aide.

Campiello Widman was full of people going and coming in the dusk of evening, women on their way to the brightly lighted shops on the Strada Nuova, a man tramping along with a ladder on his shoulder, children playing in the street, a pair of lost Americans gazing at a map, holding it up to the remains of the daylight.

Henchard drove his cart through the middle of the little square at top speed. The Americans stared, the man with the ladder turned his head, the children elbowed each other and snickered, the women stopped to watch the man in the drenched business suit pushing a *carretto* in such a hurry with such a wild tintinnabulation of bells.

To Henchard they were merely obstructions in his way. He stopped in sudden jerks to let them pass, then pushed ahead, then slowed down again to make a succession of quick turns. At the Rio di Ca' Widman a short length of the canal was blocked off with heavy plates of rusty corrugated iron. Henchard glanced down with pitying scorn at the wretched men working in the slimy ooze of the bottom, shoveling mud into wheelbarrows, carrying on the perpetual job of clearing Venetian waterways of silt because their ruthless foreman, the engineer from the Ministry of Public Works, had ordered them back to work.

Beside the empty canal the *fondamenta* was obstructed by wooden trestles. There was hardly room to get by, and the cart kept wobbling dangerously to one side.

✄

Mary and Homer Kelly were crowded together in the small cabin of the powerboat of the Nucleo Natanti in the company of three men in the smart dark uniforms of the carabinieri. The brigadier capo was at the wheel, sending the little craft whizzing under the Rialto Bridge into the Rio del Fontego dei Tedeschi. The staring headlight illuminated the turn into Rio de San Lio, the engine slowed and speeded up again, sending bow waves slapping against the Church of Santa Maria dei Miracoli. The brigadiere was making a shortcut in the direction of Rio dei Gesuiti, where Mary's finger had come down so firmly on the map. *Here,* she had said, *try here.*

They never made it to Rio dei Gesuiti. "There," cried Mary, "there he is, look! The man with the cart!"

Henchard saw the glaring headlight, he heard the roar of the engine, he heard it suddenly cut, he saw the carabinieri leaping up onto the *fondamenta,* he saw Mary Kelly pointing and shouting. Panicking, he backed up and collided with one of the trestles. A gate beside the empty canal swung open.

Slowly, as in a dream, he blundered sideways and lost his balance. The cart with all its priceless treasures lurched and threatened to tip over. The tarpaulin slipped off and a magnificent volume of Caesar's *Commentaries*, adorned with the stemma of Cardinal Bessarion and illuminated with a splendid letter *I* (for *Iulius*), flew up in the air.

Homer, who sometimes didn't know his right hand from his left, reached out one long arm and caught it neatly as it came down, and the brigadiere capo snatched up the painting before it hit the ground, and the other carabinieri grasped the handles of the cart and heaved it upright, while Richard Henchard fell slowly headfirst into the muddy bottom of the canal.

# CHAPTER 51

✺

W hen the doorbell rang, only Mrs. Wellesley was at home. She came running downstairs to the street door, her alarm about Ursula turning to indignation, angry words boiling up in her head.

But it was not Ursula at the door, it was a bedraggled woman, a perfect stranger, a disheveled-looking gypsy with wild hair and a rag around her arm. *"Signora,"* said the woman in limpid Italian, *"mi chiamo Lucia Costanza. Per piacere, posso vedere il Signor Bell?"* When Mrs. Wellesley only gaped at her, Lucia said it again in English, "My name is Lucia Constanza. Please, is Mr. Bell at home?"

If Dorothea Wellesley had been a reading woman, she might have seen this meeting as a scene right out of Dickens, like the fierce encounter in *A Tale of Two Cities* between Madame Defarge and Miss Pross.

Dorothea was not a reading woman, but she recognized the extraordinary apparition at the door as a dangerous enemy. The woman looked very much like a threat to everything Dorothea held dear. At once she vowed to protect her own.

"Mr. Bell is not home," she said coldly. Then, standing squarely in the middle of the doorway, she added, "Why do you wish to see him?" It was a rude thing to say, but outrage and curiosity overwhelmed her sense of propriety.

*"Sono una collega,"* began Lucia, but then she faltered and started over in English. She gripped the rag on her arm, which was stained with blood. "I am a colleague of Doctor Bell's. I am a procurator of Saint Mark." *Or I was, before I ran away.*

Dorothea stared at Lucia, taking in the handsome face, the curling mass of wet hair, the soaked and rumpled clothing. It was worse and worse. This dangerously attractive female was asserting a powerful claim on the husband of her own dead daughter. How was she to be defied?

The estimable Miss Pross had used physical violence to overcome Madame Defarge, but brutal muscular action was beyond the ken of Dorothea Wellesley, in spite of the passionate fury of her threats against priests and popes and the archbishop of Canterbury.

Reluctantly she introduced herself as Samuel Bell's mother-in-law and the grandmother of his little daughter (in other words, as a privileged person who had a right to her presence in this house, not like some). And then at last she stood back and asked Lucia to come in.

It was not a surrender. She was prepared for battle. She would bring all her forces into it, she would play all her cards—hearts, spades, clubs, diamonds, and even, if necessary, the ace of gold.

Lucia struggled after her up the stairs. She was so tired she could barely walk across the sitting-room floor. Half fainting, she sank into a chair.

Mrs. Wellesley glowered down at her. Was the bitch putting on an act? As someone who had put on many an act herself, she recognized the symptoms. By cheating, the gypsy had won the first round in this battle of Titans. She would not win the second.

There was no time for another move. To her chagrin Mrs. Wellesley heard Sam stumping slowly up the stairs. She didn't want to let him in. She opened the door and saw him standing on the top step with Ursula, who was holding the lid of a pot in each hand.

"You bad girl," snapped Dorothea, "where have you been?" Then she said dryly to Sam, "You have a visitor."

He murmured, "Oh, no," and stepped reluctantly into the hall. At once he saw Lucia in the room beyond. She was rising slowly from her chair, and he ran to her with a cry of joy.

Lucia laughed and allowed herself to be embraced, but then she said, *"Ohi,"* and backed away, apologizing.

"Good God," said Sam, seeing the bloodstained rag. Putting his arm around her, he glanced at his mother-in-law for guidance in the household care of miscellaneous injuries, but Dorothea sniffed and turned away. It was none of *her* affair.

So Sam took Lucia into the kitchen and cared for the torn skin of her arm with warm water and disinfectant and layers of gauze bandage. "We must call a doctor," he whispered, kissing her gently.

"No, no," said Lucia. "Not yet." And together they returned to the sitting room, where Ursula beamed at them and banged her pot lids together with a crash.

For once Mrs. Wellesley failed to scold. She was in a state of shock. This was defeat, and she knew it. The battle was over before it had begun. Dorothea withdrew into the sanctuary of her bedroom. The gypsy woman's ace of hearts had trumped her ace of gold.

But Ursula was glad. She looked at the pretty lady with the curly hair and at her father, whom she had saved. Her miracle had worked. Her father was not going to die. He had told her so.

# CHAPTER 52

⚔

S lowly and haltingly, Sam and Lucia began putting together all their bits and pieces.

Sam Bell knew and loved Lucia, but he knew nothing about the treasure that had been discovered by his own physician, Doctor Richard Henchard, and seen thereafter by both Lucia and Mary Kelly.

He was also completely unaware of the turbulent history of the gold plates and candlesticks and scrolls, the painting and the five-hundred-year-old books, bundled so insanely by Doctor Henchard from one place to another and at last nearly flung into the slimy bottom of a drained canal.

Sam did not know why Lucia had disappeared from her house in the Ghetto Nuovo. He didn't yet know that Doctor Henchard had taken her away at gunpoint and imprisoned her and tried to murder her.

And of course neither Sam nor Lucia knew anything about Henchard's dangerous pursuit of Mary Kelly through high water and low, nor about his escape and recapture with the help of the Nucleo Natanti.

It wasn't until Mary and Homer knocked on the door and came hobbling in, exhilarated, worn out, and starving, that everything could be sorted out.

But first, of course, everyone had to be introduced to everyone else. Everyone, that is, but Dorothea, who had already begun packing in her bedroom, having seen the handwriting on the wall,

### *MENE, MENE, TEKEL, UPHARSIN!*
### DOROTHEA WELLESLEY,
### YOU'LL BE BETTER OFF ELSEWHERE.

Sam was in a state of solemn joy. Reasons One and Two had vanished, the logical arguments explaining why Lucia Costanza had been forbidden him from the beginning—Reason One, his illness, and Reason Two, the fact that she was married, and then the final appalling Reason Three, her disappearance. Now here she was, sitting warmly beside him while both of them struggled to maintain some sort of decorum, and Homer and Mary tried not to grin too broadly.

"Come on, Ursula, dear," said Mary, jumping up and grasping her hand. "Let's see what we can find to eat in the kitchen. And I've got some good things upstairs. Do you like pickles?"

Sam jumped up too and went to his mother-in-law's bedroom and called through the door, "Dorothea, please join us. This is a celebration."

But Mrs. Wellesley was still cowering from the dread words on her wall, YOU'LL BE BETTER OFF ELSEWHERE, and she stayed put.

They ate and drank and talked. Ursula fell asleep and Sam put her to bed. At last, when Lucia brought out her document, they were ready to listen.

It was only three pages long. They were the same three fragile handwritten pages that she had found fluttering across the floor in the room from which Henchard had so frantically removed his treasure.

She read them aloud, translating the Italian into English, pausing sometimes for the right word, then going inexorably on. Homer put down his glass and stared gravely at his knees. Mary looked soberly at the floor. Sam gazed grimly at the pattern in the rug. It was a harrowing document. Lucia read it slowly, her voice clear and without expression.

"CODICIL TO MY LAST WILL AND TESTAMENT

"*On this day, December 6, 1943, I bequeath to the named beneficiaries the following things:*

"*I. To my synagogue, the Scuola Spagnola, these ritual vessels and scrolls, which I have hidden in this place from capture by the invading forces of the German army—two Torah scrolls with crowns of gold, one Esther scroll for Purim, three Seder plates of gold, three gold Seder cups, two silver cups for Friday services, two menorahs, and three incense burners of silver gilt. These must of course be returned to the congregation for whose sake they are now to be hidden away.*

"*II. The illuminated manuscripts listed below, from the collection of Cardinal Bessarion, and the folio volume from the Aldine press are all to be donated to the Biblioteca Marciana. All three were acquired by me at public auction in Rome. They are as follows:*

"1. *From the library of Cardinal Bessarion, a trilingual Pentateuch or Torah in Greek, Latin, and Hebrew, assembled in our fashion with Genesis at the back and Deuteronomy at the front. I note that the good cardinal proclaimed his Christianity by adding the words 'ave M(ari)a' at the top of every page.*

"2. *Also from the library of Cardinal Bessarion, a Latin codex,* Caesar's Commentaries.

"3. *From the press of Aldus Manutius, Venice, 1499, a folio volume with printed text accompanied by woodcuts of obelisks, elephants, and mystic symbols, the* Hypnerotomachia Poliphili, *or* The Dream of Poliphilius.

"*III. Painting by Raphael,* Portrait of a Young Man. *Because I stole this painting from the Nazi Oberkommandant who had himself taken it from the collection of the Czartoryski Museum in Cracow, the painting is not mine. The museum's stamp is on the back. I can only suggest that if the Polish museum continues to exist after this brutal war is over, the painting should be returned to their collection. Otherwise perhaps it might become the property of the Gallerie dell'Accademia. It is not for me to say.*

"*Signatures of witnesses:*
   *Baruch Basevi*
   *Beatrice Basevi*
"*Signature of testator: Armando Levi, December 6, 1943*"

"Armando Levi!" Sam jumped up and leaned over Lucia's shoulder to look.

Homer was mystified. "Who was Armando Levi?"

"Who was Armando Levi? My God." Sam took a moment to collect himself. "Armando Levi was a highly respected doctor who committed suicide in 1943 rather than submit to being shipped off by the Nazis to a death camp." Sam's voice was shaking. He sat down again. "I've seen his grave in the Hebrew cemetery on the Lido."

Lucia said quietly, "There's more."

"Read on," said Sam.

*"I must explain how the Raphael portrait has come into my possession.*

*"Two days after the German army began occupying this city, I was invited to an evening meeting in the headquarters of Nazi Oberkommandant Helmut Greetz. I suppose I was chosen for this honor because of my position as president of the Jewish community.*

*"In accepting the invitation I was of course on my guard, but the evening began cordially enough. The Oberkommandant has settled himself comfortably in a house in Castello, long since confiscated by the Fascisti because the owners were Jews. He offered me wine, which I refused, and then talked proudly about the paintings on the wall. These works of art, he said, had accompanied him throughout the war.*

*"Among them was the Raphael portrait. The Oberkommandant bragged that it had fallen his way when the collec-*

*tion of a museum in Cracow was looted in 1940. He asked me, 'Do you not think it a masterpiece?' I said that I did. I did not express my disgust that this great Italian work should be the toy of an animal like Greetz.*

*"After these friendly overtures, the real business of the evening began. The Oberkommandant gave me writing materials and asked me to put down the location of every Venetian synagogue and make a list of all my fellow Jews. The implication was that I, too, might benefit in some material way from this simple secretarial act.*

*"When I refused, the threats began, and it became clear to me at once how grim and terrible are the times that have come upon us. I have lost all hope that we Jews may be spared. Man, woman, and child are to be rounded up from every neighborhood in the city, from every hole and corner and hiding place, and herded away to the town of Fossoli. From there they will be taken north into Germany and Poland to be interned in concentration camps and put to death.*

*"I listened in dumb despair, wanting to ask how such inhumanity could exist, how he could speak of it without revulsion. And then the phone rang in another part of the house, and to my surprise he went out of the room to answer it. At once I snatched the painting off the wall and ran out into the street.*

*"Of course I was pursued, and there was a hue and cry. But having grown up in this city, I know every twist and turn. I took off my coat to cover the painting and made my way to this place, where I have now hidden the ritual vessels of my synagogue as well as my own beloved books. Here I have deposited the Raphael. Only my friends Signor and Signora Basevi know where they are."*

Sam interrupted, murmuring, *"Sei stanca, cara?"*
She shook her head. "No, no, I'm not tired. There's only a little more."

"*The end of my life is near. I will not live to see the day in which my beloved country will be free and master of itself again, when there will at last be an end to the folly that has created such iniquity in the world and broken my heart.*

"*Armando Levi.*"

# CHAPTER 53

✄

*A*t the carabinieri station on Campo San Zaccaria, Richard Henchard sat in a chair facing the capitano of the investigative branch of the service, the Nucleo Operativo. Surrounding Henchard, looking down at him with expressionless faces, were other officers, including several from the Questura. In an obscure corner sat Mary Kelly, somber and reluctant.

Doctor Henchard was accompanied by a celebrated legal adviser from Bologna. Henchard was indignant. "What have you got against me? I found those things. I didn't steal them. All right, I've read Armando Levi's so-called will, but it makes no claim on the Titian. The Titian is mine. I found it. The will admits the fact that he stole it in the first place."

The celebrated legal adviser muttered something, and Henchard fell silent.

"It's not a Titian," corrected the capitano softly. "It's a Raphael." Everyone glanced at the picture, which hung on the wall above a table on which lay Armando Levi's five-hundred-year-old books and all his synagogue treasures.

The young man in the Raphael portrait looked at Henchard with a knowing smile. The gold of the plates and cups glittered and gleamed.

There was gold too on the hat of the capitano, a sparkling insignia with thirteen flames, each having stalwart significance—*Loyalty! Readiness! Courage!*

"These things," said the capitano, waving his hand at the table, *"non sono importanti."* He stood up and offered his chair to a distinguished-looking broad-shouldered man with four gold stars on the shoulders of his uniform. "Generale Palma of the polizia has issued a report. Generale?"

From her corner Mary listened to the general's report. It was interrupted again and again by the sharp objections of the expensive legal adviser from the law courts of Bologna, but his complaints were ignored. With extreme courtesy the general recited an itemized list of devastating conclusions.

> "Item 1: The firearm that was at first thought to have killed Signor Lorenzo Costanza, the handgun bearing the fingerprints of his wife Lucia, was not, after all, the weapon that fired the fatal shot. The cartridge extracted from Costanza's skull is indeed the right size, but the scratches do not match those inside the barrel of the gun in question, which, in fact, shows few signs of having been fired at all. They match instead the scratches in the barrel of the weapon found on the person of Doctor Henchard at the time of his arrest by Brigadiere Capo Cardoso in the drained canal of Rio di Ca' Widman.

> "Item 2: The firing scratches in the barrel of Henchard's firearm also match the marks on the cartridge removed from the wall of a house on Calle de la Madonna, corroborating the story of Signora Kelly.

> "Item 3: They also match the cartridge found on the floor of a room in the same house, supporting the testimony of Dottoressa Lucia Costanza.

> "Item 4: The blood on the cartridge, as well as other blood samples taken from that room, match that of the dottoressa."

Mary wanted to go home. Surely this was enough. But there was more. The general and his colleagues had been even more thorough.

> "Item 5: In a search of the entire premises of the apartment rented by Doctor Henchard on the Rio della Sensa, the

*storage room on the ground floor was closely examined. This chamber is commonly occupied by the carts used by the local spazzini to collect the rubbish of the neighborhood. Vice Brigadiere Gozzoli remembered the recent disappearance of a young man employed by the Nettezza Urbana. In an interview with other spazzini he learned that the young man worked in this part of Cannaregio, and that this was the same storage room from which he set out every morning to clear the streets.*

*"Item 6: It was evident that the room had been subjected to a thorough cleaning, using a caustic substance and a brand of disinfectant employed exclusively in hospitals. Of course no purification of that kind could eliminate evidence in the fissures and cracks examined by our team of forensic pathologists. They found blood and tissue and fragments of bone. We are convinced that they come from the body of the missing spazzino."*

At this point, Henchard's Bolognese counsel erupted out of his chair in a burst of wrath.

Mary was tired of turning Italian into English in her head. Instant translation required the keenest attention. It was coming at her too fast. She gave up, and let the deep basso phrases of the general roll over her. It was like listening to Dante's *Inferno*. The details of the young *spazzino*'s death were obviously abominable.

At last it was over. The capitano maggiore took off his hat, breathed on the flames of his gold insignia, and polished them with his sleeve. Generale Palma gathered up his papers. Richard Henchard was conducted out of the room in the company of his attorney. Mary looked at Henchard bravely, but she dreaded meeting his eye. He walked proudly past her, staring straight ahead.

She stood up to leave. At once Palma came forward to thank her for leading the Nucleo Natanti to the place where Henchard had been taken. The stars on the general's shoulders glittered, his mustachioed face was awe-inspiring. *"Ah,"* said Generale Palma, *"l'intuizione delle donne!"*

"Women's intuition?" Mary shook her head. "No, no, it's nothing like that. My husband is the one with intuition, only his comes from—what? The Oversoul, I guess."

"The Oversoul?" The general looked puzzled. "You mean, from God?"

"Well, no, not exactly *God.*"

He beamed at her again, his mustachios quivering. "And you, *cara mia,* from what source does your inspiration come?"

"Well, I don't know. I guess I just think."

"Think?" There was a burst of laughter. With an old-fashioned gesture the general took her hand and kissed it.

She didn't know whether to be complimented or insulted.

⚏

Afterward she told Homer as much as she could remember.

"When they explained how he got rid of the body of the poor street cleaner I lost track. I gather it was pretty gruesome."

"What did he do, saw up the poor kid and dispose of the dismembered bits and pieces?"

Mary shuddered. "I'm afraid so."

"My poor darling." Homer put his arms around her and held her close, refraining from rubbing it in—*And this is the guy you went to bed with?*

She pulled away. "You should have heard the violent objections of Henchard's attorney."

"They won't give up easily, I guess. They'll fight all the way. Mary, dear, I hope you don't have to testify. We're supposed to go home in a couple of weeks."

"Oh, Homer, that's right." She gave him a worried look. "Homer, dear, I hope you won't mind too much. After all, you're not really a Renaissance scholar, you know you're not. Henry Thoreau and the transcendentalists, that's your bailiwick. We've got to go back to Concord, Massachusetts, and the river and the woods and the pond. It's too bad, but you'll have to face it."

"It's all right." Homer smiled a little sadly. "This has been like looking through a door from one room into another, and the other room is magnificent and full of fascination, but then you close the door and turn back to the warm fire on your own hearth. It's all right. I don't mind. I'm ready to go home."

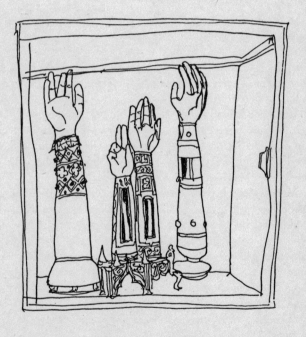

*These reliquaries in the Treasury of the Basilica of Saint Mark enclose the arm bones of saints.*

# CHAPTER 54

⚔

"Mrs. Kelly," said Ursula, smiling at Mary, "I want to show you."

"Show me?" said Mary, allowing herself to be tugged along. "Show me what?"

"You'll see." Ursula took Mary into her bedroom. Mary had been there before. They had sat together on Ursula's bed, snipping scraps of velvet and gold braid, making dresses for Ursula's doll.

But this had nothing to do with the doll. Ursula went to the bed, felt under the mattress, took out a small key, and unlocked the door of the narrow cupboard between the windows that overlooked the street. With a dramatic sweep of her arm, she threw open the cupboard doors and said, *"Ecco!"*

Mary stared. She was speechless. Ursula had created an altar inside the cupboard. She had covered the shelves with white napkins for the display of a collection of shiny ceramic images. They were holy figures, small and crudely painted. Proudly Ursula named them—the Virgin Mary, Saint Anne, Saint Mark, Saint Clare, Saint Catherine of Alexandria, Saint Catherine of Siena, Saint Joseph, Saint Francis, Saint Martin, Saint Teresa of Avila, Saint Anthony Abbot.

"Ursula, they're lovely. It's like a real church. Do you pray to them?"

Ursula nodded, beaming, and then she whispered, "Wait, there's something else."

She took Mary's hand again and led her upstairs to her father's bedroom. "Look," she said, going to Sam's bed, "they're right here." She patted the pillow and turned to Mary with a triumphant smile.

"I don't understand."

The little girl pulled off the white pillowcase and pointed to the side seam of the pillow.

At once Mary recognized the child's clumsy stitches. "You made it?" she said, bewildered. "You made a pillow for your father?"

Ursula shook her head. Smiling, she picked at the threads and pulled at a loose end. The seam parted and something fell out. Ursula picked it up and showed it to Mary. It was a small piece of wood. Groping inside the pillow her fingers found another.

"But what are they?" said Mary. And then she guessed. "Oh, Ursula, they're not—?"

"Yes," said Ursula, "they're pieces of the True Cross. Wait." She groped in the pillow again, and brought out a small bone. "It's from a saint," she said, holding it up for Mary to see.

They were the missing relics. Mary was stunned. Sam had not carelessly mislaid them, nor had his blaspheming, image-smashing, pope-burning mother-in-law stolen them. The thief was his own pious little daughter. "But why, Ursula dear," said Mary faintly, "why?"

"They made him better," said Ursula simply. "The doctor said he was going to die. But now he's perfectly all right. They were in his pillow. They saved him."

"Your father was ill?" *Of course, of course, he had been ill. She should have guessed, she should have known it all the time. She had been blind.*

"It was a secret," said Ursula. "I heard the doctor on the phone."

"So you took the relics and sewed them into his pillow, is that it?"

Ursula nodded proudly. "And the saints. They helped too."

"The saints? You mean the ones in the cupboard?"

Reverently Ursula recited their names. "Saint Catherine of Alexandria who was tortured on the wheel, Saint Catherine of Siena who had nail holes in her feet, Saint Francis whose brother and sister were the sun and moon."

"Of course." Mary looked at the little girl's small fists, still tightly closed around the pieces of the True Cross and the saintly bone. Perhaps the child was right. Perhaps it was really true that they had saved her father from a profound kind of trouble. It was certainly true that they could save him from another. "Ursula, your father is well now. You don't need them anymore. Won't you give them back?"

Ursula handed them over without a word.

1309
1806-1929

# CHAPTER 55

✄

Accompanied by Homer Kelly and a guard from the carabinieri, Sam took the relics back at once to Father Urbano in San Marco. The reliquary from the Scuola di
San Giovanni Evangelista looked as whole and entire and beautiful as it appeared in the paintings of its miracles in the Accademia. The relic of the cross showed clearly through the sparkling
new pieces of crystal.

Father Urbano rejoiced to see everything back safe and
sound, especially the reliquary. "You're well within the month
they allowed you. I'll send it over to the *scuola* right away." He
grinned and heaved a sigh of relief. "I gather there was a certain
amount of controversy over there after I talked them into letting
it go."

Sam smiled. He did not explain how thoroughly the controversy had been justified.

"And this is the lost piece of *sacro legno* from the treasury?"
said Father Urbano. "Come on. We'll put it back."

From the sacristy they walked across the basilica in a rain of
gold, under the Ascension dome, where Christ Pantocrator
ruled heaven and earth, under the four rivers of paradise, and
under the four evangelists working busily on their Gospels—
Matthew, Mark, Luke, and John.

As they moved through one sacred precinct after another, Father Urbano unhooked a succession of velvet ropes and hooked
them again with care. In the Treasury he swept Homer and Sam
into the room on the left, where the bones of saints were en-
shrined in glass and in reliquaries made of brass.

They watched as he unlocked a display case, removed an empty goblet, and dropped into it the last little piece of the True Cross. *"Eccolo!"* said Father Urbano, his smile stretching from ear to ear. The truth was, the poor priest had been lying awake at night, imagining the storm of terrible consequences that would follow if every one of the missing relics should not be returned—consequences to the cardinal patriarch himself, to the Basilica of San Marco, and of course to a humble priest whose name was Niccolò Urbano.

Homer and Sam made noises of gratification.

"And now," said the priest, looking earnestly at Sam, "you must tell me what you found out. I'm eager to know how our relics fared under your examination. Do you think any of them are genuine?"

Sam looked around the small room at all the holy relics—the rock thrown at Christ, the thorns from his crown, the sleeve-shaped reliquaries for the arm bones of saints, the great reliquary chest containing the leg bones of Saint Peter.

"I'm sorry, Father," said Sam. "I don't know. I decided not to try."

Father Urbano's mouth opened in astonishment. "You mean you didn't examine them at all?"

"Hardly at all. I stopped. I gave up."

"You gave up!" Father Urbano grinned. "Well, I confess I'm glad."

They left him at the sacristy door and made their way out of the basilica into the sunlit square. The high-water platforms were still there, but now they were benches for tired tourists from Morocco, basking in the sunshine, and a Chinese family eating sandwiches from a bag, and a couple of perspiring fashion models in fur coats posing for a photographer. The bell in the Campanile began to ring for noon.

Sam said, "Listen, Homer, there's one more thing. There's something I want to show you. It's not far away."

"Well, certainly. What is it?"

"You'll see." Sam took Homer on a ten-minute peregrination

along narrow lanes and over bridges, and halted at last before a church that was unfamiliar to Homer.

He was mystified. "What's this?"

"Let's go inside," muttered Sam. "The thing I want to show you, it's inside."

He pushed open a heavy outside door and an inner door, and at once they found themselves in a typical Venetian church with chapels and pedimented altarpieces and a painted ceiling. Homer looked up at the saints frolicking on their painted clouds. It was a riot of tumbling pink bodies with outstretched arms and naked legs dangling earthward in three-point perspective. Homer whispered to Sam, "They had more arms and legs in those days."

Sam pulled nervously at Homer's arm. "This way. It's back here." He hurried ahead of Homer toward the east end of the church, where a pair of huge paintings flanked the altar. Sam nodded at them and murmured, "Tintoretto."

"Very nice," said Homer politely, wondering what on earth was the matter with his distinguished friend, the curator of rare books in the Biblioteca Marciana.

"Here we are," whispered Sam. He stopped and folded his arms.

Homer stopped too. Three women were kneeling before a railing, their hands clasped in prayer. Before them rose a tall pedestal supporting a gold frame. Within the frame, behind a sheet of glass, hung a square of blue cloth.

*"Il Velo della Vergine,"* said Sam softly.

"Of course, I've heard of it. The Virgin's Veil."

Homer looked at it, and the more he looked, the more strangely familiar it became. Hadn't he seen that same gauzy pale blue fabric quite recently, in fact just the other day, right there in Sam's house on Salizada del Pignater?

"Sam," he began, but his friend held a finger to his lips and took his arm. As they turned away, Homer saw one of the praying women rise, kiss her fingers, and touch the frame around the sacred veil.

In the middle of Campo Santo Spirito, Sam let go of Homer's

arm and looked him in the eye and made his confession. "It's a fake."

"A fake? The Veil of the Virgin is a fake?"

"I made it myself. Ursula was making doll dresses out of one of her old frocks, so I cut a piece out of the dress myself. Then I cobbled up a frame and put the whole thing inside the door of the church with an anonymous note explaining what it was and how it had survived for two thousand years."

Homer held up an inspired hand. "Aha, I know! The First Crusade! Captured from the infidel! Carried away by sea! The ship sank! The veil was caught in a fisherman's net!"

Sam laughed ruefully. "Exactly. It was just like that. And the dear innocent priests fell for it. They were thrilled to have their very own relic. So it was just as I hoped. I wanted to exploit the gullibility of people who are so eager to believe anything, anything at all, and then I wanted to show it up as a fake."

"Hmm," said Homer, "didn't I hear that your fake is performing miracles of healing?"

"Oh, yes, and at first I was delighted about that. I thought it would be all the more crushing when I told the truth. I thought I'd be abolishing superstition with one blow. But now—God, Homer, I just don't know."

Homer laid a hand on Sam's arm. "Don't do it."

"Yes, that's what I've been thinking. I should just let it go. That's what Lucia thinks."

"She's right."

"But that means"—Sam shook his head in bewildered embarrassment—"it means it will be believed in for years. People might go on taking it seriously forever."

"Well, what's so bad about that?"

Sam looked befuddled. "Well, nothing, I guess. Not really."

❈

Mrs. Wellesley couldn't stand it. Sam's overflowing happiness was an affront to her moral dominance in the household as the mother of his late wife. It was also an insult to Henrietta in her grave.

Abandoning the field, she went to live with her sister in Milan, after packing up every one of her fiery works of art and claiming as family heirlooms all the silver flatware.

But Lucia had plenty of knives and forks. Sam and Ursula shifted their belongings to her house on the street of gardens in San Polo, near the Ponte dei Scalzi.

"You're coming with us, of course," said Lucia firmly to Mary and Homer.

*"Assolutamente,"* agreed Sam.

"But we're about to leave for Boston," protested Homer.

"And we'd surely be in the way," said Mary.

"No, no," said Lucia. Taking Mary aside, she pleaded with her. "Oh, please come. I need you to teach me how to talk to Sam's little girl. I don't know anything about children."

"But I don't have any children myself." Then Mary groaned, thinking of her long and grueling experience as the aunt of an aggravating young genius named Bennie, and his older brother John, the arachnologist, and their harum-scarum sister Annie, who had driven them so crazy last year. "Well, it's true, I do have nieces and nephews."

And therefore Homer and Mary made the move too, bringing along their half-packed suitcases.

As always at the end of a journey there were too many things

to wedge into the bags, too many guidebooks and museum catalogs and presents for nephews and nieces. And then at the last
minute Mary appeared with something else, a large mysterious
object tightly wrapped in paper and tape.

"My God," said Homer, staring at it, "what's that?"

"Oh, nothing," mumbled Mary. "It's just—well, it's a mirror." She laid it on the bed and unwrapped it. The mirror was
large and ornate, bristling with ornamental gold arabesques, a
thing as unlike his wife's normal tastes as anything Homer had
ever seen.

He gaped at it. "But, Mary dear, it won't match anything in
our house. It won't go with the river or the Canada geese or the
cattails. And how in hell will we get it home? It's too big."

"I'll carry it in my arms," promised Mary, close to tears. "I
like it, Homer. I mean, it will remind me of Venice every day for
the rest of my life."

So the mirror was one of the half-packed things to be lugged
on board a vaporetto and transported to Lucia's house in San
Polo. And there, half settled in, living out of their suitcases for
the last few days of their Venetian holiday, Mary was pleased to
watch the befriending of little Ursula by Lucia.

At first Mary had worried that the child might never come
out from under the dire influence of her grandmother Wellesley.
She wondered aloud to Homer, "Do you think the poor little
kid is doomed? Will she ever get over it?"

"You forget," said Homer. "There are anti-mentors as well as
mentors. If an anti-mentor says something's wrong, you know
it's right. Mrs. Wellesley was very useful in her way."

"I see," said Mary. "Well, good. I hope Lucia can handle it. I
don't know how she'll connect with a little girl. She's such an
important dignitary and scholar."

But then Mary was amused to discover that Lucia had a talent
for something other than civic administration. She was an expert
in the old-fashioned domestic arts of sewing and embroidery,
skills learned from her grandmother. "No man will marry you,"

Lucia's grandmother had warned her, "without a trousseau, *un corredo da sposa.*"

It had been a long time since *corredi da sposa* were in fashion in Venice, but under her grandmother's guidance Lucia had laboriously created one, and she had forgotten nothing. She taught Ursula to crochet squares in colored wool and make embroidered lazy-daisy stitches in the corners of handkerchiefs. She took her to morning mass in the Church of Santa Maria Gloriosa dei Frari. She teased her gently in English and Italian. She found her a new school.

Ursula's sad little face brightened and turned pink. At school she found a friend, and at once she and Maria were inseparable. They giggled behind Ursula's bedroom door. One day Lucia found them playing with Ursula's saints. The little figures were lined up in a wedding procession on the floor, where Saint Francis was marrying Saint Clare.

# CHAPTER 57

✣

O f course Richard Henchard lost his treasure.

The Bessarion manuscripts now belonged to the city of Venice, as the great cardinal himself had long ago intended. Sam welcomed the two heavy volumes into the Biblioteca Marciana with pomp and ceremony, along with the Aldine *Dream of Poliphilius*, another great prize.

The Raphael painting was handed over to the Accademia, at least temporarily. But when the superintendent discovered to her chagrin that the Cracow museum still existed, the one from which the painting had originally been taken by the Germans in 1940, she had to give it up.

The curator of the Polish museum went out of his mind with joy. He called the superintendent and raved ecstatically in three languages. "The last of the three! It's the last of the three!"

The superintendent held the phone away from her ear, wishing the man would control his gloating rapture. "The three? What three?"

"The Germans took three favorites from our collection for themselves, a Leonardo, a Rembrandt, and a Raphael. The first two came back to us after the war, but the Raphael was never found. Thank God we have it at last! Our magnificent Raphael! Praise be to God!"

*And to me,* thought the Accademia superintendent a little sourly. *After all, I did not have to be so generous. I could have kept it right here in Italy where it belongs.*

There was no question about the ritual vessels and the Torah scrolls. They were to be returned at once to Armando Levi's own synagogue, the Scuola Spagnola in the Ghetto Vecchio. The Venetian newspaper, *Il Gazzettino*, made much of the story.

"Look at this," said Homer, "there's going to be a special service." He showed Mary a photograph of one of the candlesticks on the front page. *"Una cerimonia di celebrazione."*

Downstairs they could hear Lucia calling good-bye to Ursula. Mary glanced out the window and saw her wave as Ursula trotted away to school. She heard Sam call, "Lucia?" He was about to go off for the day himself, commuting by vaporetto along the entire length of the Grand Canal, all the way to San Marco and the Marciana. Mary saw Lucia hurry back into the house to say good-bye. There followed a long and tender silence.

Mary poured coffee from the electric pot. "When is the celebration? Do you think we could go?"

"Um—*il sabato ebraico, Novembre 23,* that's tomorrow." Homer folded the newspaper and sipped his coffee. "Sure we can go. Why not? For heaven's sake, you deserve to be there. If it weren't for you, that bastard would have melted everything down by now. Think of it, all that gold."

Mary picked up the paper. There was another picture, a sixty-year-old photograph of Doctor Armando Levi, and an article with a heading in large print,

ARMANDO LEVI,
EROE EBREO,
VENEZIA 1943

"What's *eroe?*" asked Mary, frowning.

Homer looked at her pityingly. "It means hero. Armando Levi, Jewish hero."

"Oh, of course." Mary looked up. "Homer, I've just thought of something. Why didn't the two people who witnessed his will come back to the hiding place after the war and rescue everything?"

Homer was about to drink his coffee. He put down his cup. "Can't you guess why?"

"Oh, oh, of course. How terrible." Mary jumped up and hurried into the bedroom. Rummaging in a suitcase, tumbling the contents this way and that, she found the book she was looking for. When she picked it up, the torn pieces of her snapshot of Richard Henchard fell out and fluttered to the floor. She picked them up and tossed them in the wastebasket. Then she took the book to Homer at the breakfast table.

"There's a list," she said, turning to the last few pages. "This is the book I bought in the Hebrew Museum. It's got a list of all the Venetian Jews who were deported." Homer watched as she ran her finger down the page. Then her finger stopped, and she read aloud the names of the two witnesses to Armando Levi's will. "Baruch Basevi and Beatrice Basevi."

"So they were taken away," murmured Homer sadly, "before they could tell anyone else."

Mary slammed the book shut. "Listen, Homer, I know we've got to finish packing, but there's something else we've got to do first."

⋈

The Hebrew cemetery was on the Lido. They took a vaporetto across the lagoon.

The iron gates of the cemetery were closed, but when they rang the doorbell a caretaker came at once and let them in. In answer to Homer's question he looked thoughtful. *"La tomba di Armando Levi?"* Then he grinned. *"Sì! Penso sia possibile trovarla. Seguitemi, per favore."*

"What did he say?" murmured Mary, as the caretaker turned his back and walked away.

"He thinks he can find it. Come on."

It was a beautiful cemetery. The gravestones were set among tall cypresses. Mary and Homer walked along the narrow paths after the caretaker, stopping occasionally to see stones dedicated to other victims of Nazi extermination. *"Non sono tombe,"* said the caretaker. *"Solo monumenti commemorativi."*

This time they both understood. These were not graves, only

memorials, because there had been no bodies to bury. These people had never come back.

Levi's monument was a grave. The caretaker left them looking down at the flat stone.

At first the inscription seemed illegible. The letters were half-covered with lichen. Mary knelt and ran her finger over them, deciphering a word here and there about the sorrow of sons and daughters, the grief of the city of Venice. The sense of a timeless tragedy crept up into her hand through the spreading moss and the patches of yellow lichen.

*In every synagogue in Venice a lamp is lit before the Holy Ark. Within stands the Torah, inscribed with the first five books of the Bible.*

# CHAPTER 58

⌘

Next day was Saturday, the Jewish Sabbath, the day of the ceremonial return of Armando Levi's treasure to the Scuola Spagnola.

People were pouring into the synagogue. "Ah, yes, I recognize the doorway," said Homer. "It's the one in your picture."

They were met on the doorstep by the chief rabbi. He beamed at Mary. "Ah, signora, we have met before. Permit me to thank you"—he paused, having used up all his prepared English remarks, and finished in Italian—"*personalmente, con sincerità profondissima.*" He clasped her hand and shook Homer's vehemently up and down.

Modestly they followed him in the door, to be introduced to smiling members of the congregation. One was a very old man who remembered Armando Levi.

Haltingly Mary tried to say she wished Doctor Levi had lived to be with them today, but the old man shook his head and said in his weak old voice, *"No, no. Dottor Levi era molto vecchio nel 1943."* He threw up his frail hands. *"Oggi avrebbe centoquaranta anni."*

Homer was bending far down to listen. He nodded with exaggerated wobbles of his head to show he understood. "He'd be one hundred and forty years old! My goodness!"

"Look, Homer," whispered Mary, nodding at the display of Armando Levi's golden treasures, now brought so triumphantly back into the synagogue from which they had been removed more than half a century before. They sparkled on a table, the plates leaning upright, the cups and menorahs gleaming and glistening, the silver pennants of the spice boxes blowing east, west, north, and south.

Mary and Homer moved on into a magnificent high chamber, sat down in one of the side-facing pews, and looked up at the splendor of the glittering chandeliers and the tall windows.

There was a rustle as everyone stood up, and a general soft murmur and a jingling of bells. Mary stuck her elbow into Homer and whispered, "Here they come."

At first the golden dazzle was blinding, as the procession of rabbis approached in a flood of sunlight. Then the dazzle diminished until it was only the familiar brilliance of the tall crowns of the Torah scrolls. They too had found their way home at last.

The service began with chanting and singing. In their shawls the men of the congregation stood sideways and bowed toward the Ark. After a prayer of thanksgiving by the chief rabbi, there were speeches by dignitaries honoring the memory of Armando Levi. Then the members of the congregation turned the pages of their prayer books, chanting in Hebrew. There was more singing and chanting.

Homer's mind was elsewhere. It was a grimmer elsewhere. He was trying to tie together the two loose and fraying ends of a cord. Armando Levi was at one end, along with the synagogue in which they were sitting and the whole history of the Jews in Venice. At the other end dangled the relics of the True Cross.

Tied together, the two ends made a circle. It was not a pretty circle, not a wreath of fruit and flowers. Woven into the story of the crucifixion of the man called Jesus Christ were two thousand years of anti-Semitic persecution.

That was the circle. The Christian relics, those precious fragments that had been so long regarded as miraculous in healing, were like accusing fingers. For two thousand years Jews had been herded into ghettos and thrown out of Christian countries and tormented and put to death because of a grisly misunderstanding. *Matthew, Mark, Luke and John, bless the bed that I lie on, and damn the Jews, please, at the same time.*

Homer remembered the open mouths of the singers in the monastic church of the Frari, he remembered the words echoing from the walls and rebounding from the vaulted ceiling, *Let him be crucified, let him be crucified. His blood be on us, and on our children.*

For whatever reason, and Homer knew there were historical reasons for the crude violence of the Gospel accounts of the trial before Pilate, those very same Gospels had been like a curse echoing down the ages, condemning the Jews of the world to centuries of suffering, as though Jesus had not been a Jew himself but a pink and prosperous Christian.

"Get up, Homer," whispered Mary.

"Oh, right," mumbled Homer, and he got to his feet because everyone else was standing. But he hadn't yet carried his thought to its conclusion. Staring dreamily at the reverent faces on the other side of the splendid room, he decided that Venice carried both things on her back, not only her hundred beautiful Christian churches but also this Hebrew ghetto created by the might of the Christian Republic, this island neighborhood that had once imprisoned its people like beasts. And of course that was why Shakespeare's Shylock had felt the need to proclaim his humanity—*Hath not a Jew eyes? If you prick us, do we not bleed?*

The service was nearly over. The rabbi unrolled one of the recovered Torah scrolls a few inches, and began reading aloud in Hebrew, using a silver pointer to follow the line—

*"BERESHIS BARA ELOHIM ET HASHAMAYIM VE ET
HAÄRETZ."*

Homer beamed with pride, because he knew what it was, it was the first chapter of Genesis, because the rabbi was reading the line from right to left at the *end* of the scroll, which was really the *beginning,* because the Torah went *backward* with Deuteronomy at the front and Genesis at the back, and therefore Homer

knew exactly what the Hebrew words meant because the first five
books of the Bible belonged to both Jews and Christians alike—

*IN THE BEGINNING, GOD CREATED THE HEAVENS
AND THE EARTH.*

Everyone beamed. Eyes were wet. The rabbi covered the
scroll in a velvet garment and carried it solemnly in procession
with the other rabbis. The bells on the crowns and finials of all
the Torahs jangled and clanged. Men reached out their shawls
to the velvet coverings, then reverently lifted the knotted ends to
their eyes and lips. There was more chanting and singing, and
the service was over.

Mary and Homer moved out of the Scuola Spagnola in a
friendly crowd. To their surprise they found the celebration con-
tinuing outside. Young men were joining hands and dancing.
Their pace was slow and solemn, two steps forward, one step
back, around and around.

Perhaps, thought Mary, the tramp of their dancing feet was
shaking the pilings under the entire city of Venice, trembling the
withered toes of Saint Catherine of Siena, ruffling the Veil of the
Virgin, knocking together the saintly bones in the Treasury of
Saint Mark. Well, of course that was silly, but dancing was a
wonderful kind of worshiping.

Why didn't they dance in the First Parish Church in Con-
cord, Massachusetts, instead of gazing at their shoes in prayer?
What about all those other places where she had sat beside
Homer on a Sunday morning?

They had listened, agreed, disagreed, and sung hymns, but
they had never danced in Old West Church in Nashoba, or in
the Church of the Commonwealth in Boston, or in Quaker
Meeting in Nantucket, or in Memorial Church at Harvard, or in
the University Church of Saint Mary the Virgin in Oxford, or
in the Cathedral of Florence, and of course most especially they
had not danced at Walden Pond, which in spite of its eroded
banks and trampled hillsides, in spite of its sunbathers and hik-

ers and tourists, was a kind of church. It was another place where you could prod awake a wisp of devotional feeling. All it needed was a little dancing.

☙

And so they left for home.

The sensible way to get to the mainland would have been to take the train. Instead they counted their remaining lire and splurged on a water taxi that carried them down the whole length of the Grand Canal.

"Look, Homer," said Mary, as the lagoon opened out before them, with the domes of San Marco rising like puddings beyond the Campanile. "Say good-bye to Santa Maria della Salute!"

Homer looked at the great domed church affectionately as the taxi streaked past it, neatly maneuvering between a pair of vaporetti—one going, one coming—and dodging a gondola floating like gossamer.

The gondola was carrying the party of English visitors who had been on holiday in Venice at the same time as the Kellys, visiting the same tourist sites under the same pellucid sky, poising their umbrellas against the same rain, splashing through the same high-rising tides. They too were ready to go home (all but the wife of the bishop, who had not finished collecting colorful observations for her Venetian novel).

"So long, good old Salute!" cried Homer, leaning far out over the spray to wave good-bye.

"Who is that man?" said Elizabeth Cluff-Luffter, staring. "He's waving. Do we know those people?"

"Surely not," said Tertius Alderney, member of Parliament from the Channel Isles.

"Americans, I think," sniffed Louise Alderney.

"I never saw them before in my life," said the bishop of Seven Oaks.

But the great church of the Salute seemed to know them. It turned on its hexagonal bottom as though keeping them in sight. Greedily they watched it float away behind them, relishing its Venetian double nature—because Santa Maria della Salute was not only an architectural marvel, it was a piece of fantasy, a fat round temple rising from the sea, its dome alive with springy spirals, its broad steps dropping down into the water as though Neptune himself might ascend, his long hair streaming with seaweed, his whiskers clotted with shells.

# AFTERWORD

The character known in this book as Armando Levi was inspired by a real Venetian doctor, Giuseppe Jona. Doctor Jona, president of the Hebrew community and head physician of the Ospedale Civile, was revered in Venice as the doctor of the poor, "the Hebrew saint." After the German army descended on the city in 1943, Jona committed suicide.

Signor Cesare Vivante, currently the president in Venice of the Comitato per il Centro Storico Ebraico, knew Doctor Jona very well, and compares his suicide to that of the Roman stoic, Cato of Utica. In Dante's *Divine Comedy*, Cato was the guardian of the approach to Purgatory. In life, after losing a battle to Julius Caesar, Cato was reputed to have killed himself rather than survive the death of the Roman Republic. In the *Divine Comedy*, Virgil pleads with Cato for Dante's entrance to Purgatory—

> 'Tis liberty he seeks—how dear a thing
> That is, they know who give their lives for it;
> Thou know'st; for thee this passion drew death's sting
> In Utica. . . .

The words of the last paragraph of the fictional will of Armando Levi are really the words of Doctor Jona, as given in a book documenting this period, *Gli Ebrei a Venezia, 1938–1945*, edited by Renata Segre (Venice: Cardo, 1995).

Levi's grave as it is described in chapter 57 is like that of

Giuseppe Jona in the Hebrew cemetery on the Lido. But Armando Levi's hidden collection is of course entirely fictional.

Raphael's *Portrait of a Young Man* was lost in World War II. In 1940 it was removed with many other works of art from the Czartoryski collection in Cracow. During the next two years it was shuttled back and forth between Germany and Poland in company with Leonardo's *Lady with the Ermine* and Rembrandt's *Landscape with the Good Samaritan*. After the war the Leonardo and the Rembrandt were returned to the Czartoryski Museum. The Raphael was never recovered.

The story of its disappearance and the history of what happened to other European works of art during the Second World War are vividly told in two books, *The Spoils of War,* edited by Elizabeth Simpson (Harry N. Abrams, 1997) and *The Rape of Europa* by Lynn Nicholas (Knopf, 1994).

My account of the fate of the Raphael is of course pure invention. No Torah scrolls or ritual objects are missing from the Scuola Spagnola, nor have any Aldine books or Bessarion manuscripts been added to the holdings of the Biblioteca Marciana. The Church of Santo Spirito and the Veil of the Virgin exist only in cloud-cuckoo-land.

**FOR THE BEST IN PAPERBACKS, LOOK FOR THE**

### More Homer Kelly titles from
### "today's best American mystery writer"
### —*St. Louis Post-Dispatch*

Treat yourself to Jane Langton and her Homer Kelly mysteries
with quirky suspenseful cases, in locations splendidly evoked
by her trademark line drawings. Harvard professor and retired
policeman Kelly proves his mettle in some of the cleverest,
most erudite, and funniest mysteries around.

**THE DANTE GAME**
*ISBN 0-14-013887-0*

**GOD IN CONCORD**
*ISBN 0-14-016594-0*

**DARK NANTUCKET NOON**
*ISBN 0-14-005836-2*

**GOOD AND DEAD**
*ISBN 0-14-012687-2*

**DEAD AS A DODO**
*ISBN 0-14-024795-5*

**MURDER AT THE GARDNER**
*ISBN 0-14-011382-7*

**DIVINE INSPIRATION**
*ISBN 0-14-017376-5*

**THE SHORTEST DAY**
*ISBN 0-14-017377-3*

**THE FACE ON THE WALL**
*ISBN 0-14-028157-6*

**THE TRANSCENDENTAL
MURDER**
*ISBN 0-14-014852-3*

# FOR THE BEST IN PAPERBACKS, LOOK FOR THE

In every corner of the world, on every subject under the sun, Penguin represents quality and variety—the very best in publishing today.

For complete information about books available from Penguin—including Puffins, Penguin Classics, and Arkana—and how to order them, write to us at the appropriate address below. Please note that for copyright reasons the selection of books varies from country to country.

**In the United Kingdom:** Please write to *Dept. EP, Penguin Books Ltd, Bath Road, Harmondsworth, West Drayton, Middlesex UB7 0DA.*

**In the United States:** Please write to *Penguin Putnam Inc., P.O. Box 12289 Dept. B, Newark, New Jersey 07101-5289* or call 1-800-788-6262.

**In Canada:** Please write to *Penguin Books Canada Ltd, 10 Alcorn Avenue, Suite 300, Toronto, Ontario M4V 3B2.*

**In Australia:** Please write to *Penguin Books Australia Ltd, P.O. Box 257, Ringwood, Victoria 3134.*

**In New Zealand:** Please write to *Penguin Books (NZ) Ltd, Private Bag 102902, North Shore Mail Centre, Auckland 10.*

**In India:** Please write to *Penguin Books India Pvt Ltd, 11 Panchsheel Shopping Centre, Panchsheel Park, New Delhi 110 017.*

**In the Netherlands:** Please write to *Penguin Books Netherlands bv, Postbus 3507, NL-1001 AH Amsterdam.*

**In Germany:** Please write to *Penguin Books Deutschland GmbH, Metzlerstrasse 26, 60594 Frankfurt am Main.*

**In Spain:** Please write to *Penguin Books S. A., Bravo Murillo 19, 1° B, 28015 Madrid.*

**In Italy:** Please write to *Penguin Italia s.r.l., Via Benedetto Croce 2, 20094 Corsico, Milano.*

**In France:** Please write to *Penguin France, Le Carré Wilson, 62 rue Benjamin Baillaud, 31500 Toulouse.*

**In Japan:** Please write to *Penguin Books Japan Ltd, Kaneko Building, 2-3-25 Koraku, Bunkyo-Ku, Tokyo 112.*

**In South Africa:** Please write to *Penguin Books South Africa (Pty) Ltd, Private Bag X14, Parkview, 2122 Johannesburg.*